Wisdom of Gandhi

Widom of Gandhi

Compiled by

Prashant Gupta

Ocean Books Pvt. Ltd.

ISO 9001:2015 Publishers

Published by
Ocean Books (P) Ltd.
4/19 Asaf Ali Road,
New Delhi-110 002 (INDIA)
e-mail: info@oceanbooks.in

ISBN 978-81-8430-575-3
WISDOM OF GANDHI

Edition
2026

Price
₹ 400.00 (Rupees Four Hundred only)

Printed at
Jai Laxmi Printing Press, Delhi

A brief Biography of Mahatma Gandhi

William Shakespeare said, Some are born great, some achieve greatness, and some have greatness thrust upon them.ƒ One can achieve greatness only by one s deeds and not by one s birth. Mahatma Gandhi, the father of the nation, was such a great person. Mohandas Karamchand Gandhi was called Mahatma Gandhi for his principles of non-violence, sacrifices for India s independence and the great efforts he made for societal transformation.

Mahatma Gandhi was born on October 2, 1869, at Porbandar in Rajkot, Kathiawad in Gujarat. His father, Karamchand Gandhi, the Diwan of Rajkot, was a very honest and religious-minded person. His mother, Putli Bai, was also a pious lady of refined sensibilities. His parents greatly influenced Gandhiji.

Gandhiji received his primary education in Rajkot but, at an early age of 12 years, he was married to Kasturba, a modest and religious lady.

Gandhiji was greatly influenced by his mother s ideology. He was also inspired and deeply moved by the plays: *Satyavadi Harishchandra* and *Shravan Kumar*. From an early age, he

determined to make truth and service the guiding principles of his life. Once, his elder brother had incurred a huge debt and he told Mohandas about it. Neither of them had the courage to ask their parents for the money. Finally Mohandas stole a small amount of gold from the house and paid off his brother s loan. His brother s problem was solved but Mohandas was faced with a greater problem: The theft weighed heavily on his mind and there was severe repentance in his heart. He wanted to confess his crime, but he could not utter a word. At last he wrote a letter about the entire incident and gave it to his father. He stood silently before his father for punishment, with tears rolling down his cheeks. After going through the letter his father embraced him and he was forgiven, but he had to promise that he would never do it again. And Gandhiji kept his word throughout his life.

In 1887 he passed his matriculation examination and in 1888 he went to England to study law. At that time he promised his mother that he would never touch meat, wine and women. While in England, Gandhiji also studied the many religious scriptures of other religions. After reading the English translation, he was profoundly influenced by the *Bhagwad Gita* that guided him throughout his life. He also studied the *Bible*. Teachings on non-violence in the *Bible* became one of the guiding principles of his life. It was during this time that his mother died. And in 1892, Gandhiji returned to India as a barrister and started practice in Bombay (Mumbai). Later he came to Rajkot, but was soon to leave for South Africa to fight a case on behalf of Abdullah and Company, an established firm, located in Porbandar. On reaching South Africa he found the attitude of the British very cruel towards the Indians. He

himself suffered at their hands when he was travelling in a second-class compartment. A British officer entered the compartment and ordered him to vacate his seat and move to another compartment. Gandhiji refused. The police officer forcibly evicted Gandhiji from the compartment.

Gandhiji was deeply agonized by this incident. Despite this he decided to stay on, work patiently and accomplished first the duties assigned to him. After successfully resolving the legalities of the Abdullah and Company case, he started his protest against the British Government s maltreatment of the Indians. With the assistance of the Indian community in South Africa, he formed the Natal Indian Congress . Thousands of people, both Indian and white, supported Gandhiji with enthusiasm. It was a new and unprecedented movement the British were faced with. Initially, the Government took Gandhiji s protest lightly. But soon they became alert when they realised that the movement was influencing people at large.

Gandhiji campaigned successfully against the British Government for several years in South Africa, often at the risk of his own life. This was the first victory he achieved through non-violence. Even his diehard opponents could not help being impressed by him. At that time, Gandhiji took the vow of austerity.

In 1914 he returned to India as a successful leader and an able politician and started the freedom movement along with other great leaders such as Lokmanya Tilak and Gokhale. He regarded truth and non-violence as the most powerful weapons and decided to employ them in his struggle against the British Raj. He laid the foundations of the Sabarmati Ashram near Ahmedabad for this purpose. The rules of this ashram were

very strict and applicable to all residents, but everyone, without any discrimination, was allowed to enter.

In the year 1919, Gandhiji opposed the Rowlatt Act. To protest against this act, a large crowd had gathered at Jalianwala Bagh in Amritsar when General Dwyer opened fire and killed several hundreds of innocent people assembled there. Gandhiji was deeply shocked by this incident.

Several movements were started by the Mahatma in the country to eradicate racial discrimination. At the same time, keeping in view the economic condition of the country, he started promoting the charkha, the spinning wheel, and the Khadi and village development schemes. The British could not tolerate any type of freedom and independence demanded by the Indians. Every now and then they formulated rules and regulations to suppress any aspirations the Indians might have. One of these oppressive measures was the tax suddenly levied on salt, one of the essential food items used daily by the common man. Gandhiji commenced his march to break the salt law. This march known as the Dandi March started at the Sabarmati Ashram and ended at the Dandi village on the coast near Surat. The march started on the 12th of March, 1930 and continued for 24 days. It saw people arriving in huge numbers from every corner of the country to join Gandhiji. Gandhiji was arrested by the British for breaking the salt law and imprisoned. But, he succeeded in building a feeling of confidence among the Indian people.

In 1939, the Second World War broke out and the British Government forced India into war without consulting the Indian leaders. Gandhiji strongly protested against this high handedness. Meanwhile, Congress demanded complete freedom from the British Government but the demand was ignored. In protest, Gandhiji started the Quit India Movement in 1942. He was arrested along with many others and sent to prison. During his two-year incarceration in prison, he lost his brother Mahadev, who died in 1942 and then his wife, Kasturba Gandhi passed away in 1944. On being released from prison in 1944, Gandhiji found many obstacles on the path to complete freedom. The problem of communalism was becoming grave: Hindus and Muslims, who had participated together in the struggle for freedom against the British, now became enemies because of the British policy of divide and

rule. Mohammad Ali Jinnah, President of the Muslim League, presented demand for a separate state called Pakistan. Gandhiji made strong protests against this. He went to Mumbai to request Jinnah to change his decision but Jinnah was unyielding.

Gandhiji was deeply shaken. He could not imagine a divided India. He was pained by the division of the country on the basis of religion.

On 15th August 1947, India became free under the leadership of Gandhiji. But, because of the Partition riots broke out. So, when the country was celebrating Independence Gandhiji was marching in the streets of Calcutta and Noakhali for peace, and against Hindu-Muslim riots. When he was in Noakhali, he was informed of the fierce struggle going on in the Punjab. When he reached Delhi, he found bloody riots on the roads. There seemed to be no end to the riots and the bloodshed and Gandhiji used the only weapon left to him: he started a fast unto death to make the people see reason. Ffinally the riots came to an end after much bloodshed, but left a deep and lasting animosity between the two communities and the two countries.

Gandhiji was a social worker, reformer and nation builder. he derived real pleasure in service and social reform activities. He considered his life to be a laboratory that can be used for the purpose of becoming a good person. After Independence, Gandhiji handed over the reins of the country to Pandit Jawaharlal Nehru. India had achieved freedom, but the country was faced with many challenges.Gandhiji decided to make future plans for the country but there were those who opposed his non-violent principles and liberal policies. They protested against him in many ways. On 30th January 1948 Nathuram Godse shot Gandhiji dead.

His last words were Hey Ram . News of his assassination astonished the whole world.

The life of Bapu, as Gandhiji was called, was one of dedication and sacrifice. Age-old slavery was transformed into freedom only because of his dedication and determination. Gandhiji s life was greatly influenced by Raja Harishchandra, his mother, the plays of Shravan Kumar, and learned writers such as Thoreau, Tolstoy, Rousseau, and Ruskin. His principles and the ideology of non-violence and service developed from his reading.

Gandhiji was proud of being a Hindu. He regarded the reading of *Bhagwad Gita* essential in his daily routine. He was a believer in the ideals of Ram Rajya. He tried to bring social equality by eradicating untouchability and caste discrimination. He fought for the uplift of Harijans. He tried to grant them equal rights to enter temples; he advocated for their presence at feasts, marriages and other religious celebrations and regarded untouchability as a social evil. He worked, for example, with leprosy patients who were also among the untouchables in society. He regarded service to humanity as the only aim of his life. He firmly believed that our country could only prosper if we made our villages economically independent through cottage industries.

Gandhiji not only preached but put in practice whatever he preached. Truth and non-violence were his two ideals for him, truth meant God and non-violence was another name for unlimited love. He was also a staunch supporter of the protection of the cow. He had limitless affection for children. He also worked hard to make Hindi the national language.

It is said that when Gandhiji was once on a tour of some villages, people assembled in large numbers to have his *darshan*. When he came to know that a woman could not come out to meet him because she did not have good clothes, he immediately tore half of his dhoti and sent it to her and made a promise that until this condition was solved, he would wear only half a dhoti. He kept his promise.

Mahatma Gandhi holds an important place, along with Raja Ram Mohan Roy, in the improvement of the condition of women. He believed that women were far ahead in observing the qualities of truth, non-violence and morality. He was a supporter of women s emancipation and started many programmes to bring women into the mainstream of national life.

The three fundamental ideals of education according to Gandhiji were:

1. Every student should learn a handicraft skill.
2. Education should enable self-dependence, so that anyone could use it to earn his living. It should also play an important role in character development.
3. The medium of education should be the mother tongue.

Abstinence

Abstinence is forgiveness only when there is power to punish; it is meaningless when it pretends to proceed from a helpless creature.

Abuse

The best way of losing a cause is to abuse your opponent and to trade upon his weakness.

Action

- Action for one's own self binds; action for the sake of others delivers from bondage.
- My Gita tells me that evil can never result from good action.
- What is faith worth if it is not translated into action?

Administration

You assist an administration most effectively by obeying its orders and decrees. An evil administration never deserves such allegiance.

Advaita

I believe in advaita; I believe in the essential unity of man and for that matter of all that lives.

Affliction

Every affliction has its own rich lesson to teach, if we would learn it.

Africa

The commerce between India and Africa will be of ideas and services, not of the manufactured goods against raw materials after the fashion of the Western exploiters.

Aggressor

The aggressor always had a purpose behind his attack; he wanted something to be done, some object to be surrendered by the defender.

Agriculture

- To forget how to dig the earth and tend the soil is to forget ourselves.
- Weeding is as necessary to agriculture as sowing.

Ahimsa

- Ahimsa is the highest ideal. It is meant for the brave, never for the cowardly.
- Ahimsa is the eradication of the desire to injure or to kill.
- Ahimsa is not a matter of mere dialectics: it transcends it.
- Ahimsa is the highest duty. Even if we cannot practise it in full, we must try to understand its spirit and refrain, as far as is humanly possible, from violence.
- Ahimsa means infinite love, which again means infinite capacity for suffering.
- Ahimsa is an attribute of the brave. Cowardice and ahimsa don't go together any more than water and fire.
- Ahimsa, in theory, no one knows. It is as indefinable as God.
- The highest religion has been defined by negative word: ahimsa.
- Ahimsa is one of the world's greatest principles, which no power on earth can wipe out.
- Dharma is one and one only. Ahimsa means moksha and

moksha is the realisation of truth.

- Love and ahimsa are matchless in their effect.
- Love in the sense of ahimsa had only a limited number of votaries in the world.
- Ahimsa is the attribute of the soul and, therefore, be practised by everybody in all the affairs of life.

- Ahimsa is the strongest force known.
- Ahimsa is the height of Kshatriya dharma as it represents the climax of fearlessness.
- The fullest application of ahimsa does make life impossible.
- The most distinctive and largest contribution of Hinduism to India's culture is the doctrine of ahimsa.
- True ahimsa should mean a complete freedom from ill-will and anger and hate, and an overflowing love for all.
- Ahimsa and love is one and the same thing.
- Ahimsa and Truth are so intertwined that it is practically impossible to disentangle and separate them.
- Ahimsa is my God and Truth is my God.
- Truth and ahimsa shall never be destroyed.
- The principle of ahimsa is hurt by every evil thought, by undue haste, by lying, by hatred, by wishing ill to anybody.
- Ahimsa calls for the strength and courage to suffer without retaliation, to receive blows without returning any.
- Ahimsa can be practised only towards those who are inferior to you in every way.
- Ahimsa was preached to man when he was in full vigour of life and able to look his adversaries straight in the face.
- The greater the realisation of truth and ahimsa, the greater the illumination.
- The path of truth is as narrow as it is straight. Even so is that of ahimsa.
- Use truth as your anvil, non-violence as your hammer and anything that does not stand the test when it is

brought to the anvil of truth and hammered with ahimsa, reject as non-Indian.

• The removal of untouchability is one of the highest expressions of ahimsa.

• Cow-protection can only be secured by cultivating universal friendliness, *i.e.* ahimsa.

- Ahimsa is nothing if not a well-balanced exquisite consideration of one's neighbour and an idle man is wanting in that elementary consideration.
- Ahimsa is a science. The word 'failure' has no place in the vocabulary of science.
- Ahimsa magnifies one's own defects and minimises those of the opponent. It regards the mole in one's own eye as a beam and the beam in the opponent's eye as a mole.
- Ahimsa must be placed before everything else while it is professed.
- Ahimsa must express itself through the acts of selfless service of the masses.
- Ahimsa is no mere theory with me, but it is a fact of life based on extensive experience.
- Ahimsa should not fear the secret of open hand of imperialists.
- When the Gita was written, although people believed in ahimsa and wars were not taboo, nobody observed the contradiction between wars and ahimsa.
- What it is but my ahimsa that draws thousands of women to me in fearless confidence.
- Truth is my religion and ahimsa is the only way of its realisation.
- Truth and ahimsa demand that no human being may debar himself from serving any other human being, no matter how sinful he may be.
- One who hooks his fortune to ahimsa, the law of love, daily lessens the circle of destruction and to that extent promotes life and love.
- My anekantavada is the result of the twin doctrine of satya and ahimsa.

- When two nations are fighting, the duty of a votary of ahimsa is to stop the war.
- My ahimsa would not tolerate the idea of giving a free meal to a healthy person who has not worked for it in some honest way.
- Ahimsa and truth are as my two lungs. I can't live without them.
- My errors have been errors of calculation and judging men, not in appreciating the true nature of truth and ahimsa or in their application.
- Indeed, these errors and my prompt confessions have made me surer of my insight into the implications of truth and ahimsa.
- All my experiments in ahimsa have taught me that non-violence in practice means common labour with the body.
- Whatever strength the masses have is due entirely to ahimsa, however imperfect or defective its practice might have been.
- True ahimsa should wear a smile even on death bed brought about by an assailant. It is only with that ahimsa that we can befriend our opponents and win their love.
- If ahimsa is not of the brave but of the weak, and if it will bend the knee before himsa, Gandhism deserves to be destroyed.
- The alphabet of ahimsa is best learnt in domestic school and I can say from experience that if we secure success there, we are sure to do so everywhere else.
- A votary of ahimsa always prays for ultimate deliverance from the bondage of flesh.
- A steadfast pursuit of ahimsa is inevitably bound to truth, not to violence.
- I see clear breach of ahimsa even in driving away the monkeys; the breach would be proportionately greater if they have to be killed.
- A votary of ahimsa cannot subscribe to the utilitarian formula (of the greatest good of the greatest number).

He will strive for the greatest good of all and die in the attempt to realise the ideal.

- Woman is the incarnation of ahimsa. (Ahimsa means infinite love, which again means infinite capacity for suffering.)
- Woman is more filled than man to make exploration and take bolder action in ahimsa.
- Khadi has been conceived as the foundation and the image of ahimsa. A real khadi-wearer will not utter an untruth. A real khadi-wearer will harbour no ill-will, no violence, no deceit, no impurity.
- In swaraj, based on ahimsa, people need not know their rights, but it is necessary for them to know their duties.
- No power on earth can subjugate you when you are armed with the sword of ahimsa. It ennobles both the victor and the vanquished.
- The votary of ahimsa has only one thought in mind that is, of God.
- The votary of ahimsa must cultivate a habit of uremitting toil, sleepless vigilance and ceaseless self-control.
- The richest grace of ahimsa will descend easily upon the owner of hard discipline.
- Love, otherwise ahimsa, sustains this planet of ours.
- In an atmosphere of ahimsa, one has no scope to put his ahimsa to the test. It can be tested only in the face of himsa.
- A soldier fights with an irresistible strength when he has blown up his bridges and burnt his boats. So it is with a soldier of ahimsa.
- Man lives freely by his readiness to die, if need be, at the hands of his brother, never by killing him.
- The strength to kill is not essential for self-defence; one ought to have the strength to die.
- If the lambs of the world had been willingly led, they would have long ago saved themselves from the butcher's knife.
- If the circulation of blood theory could not have been

discovered without vivisection, the human kind could well have done without it.

- The scriptures of the Christians, the Muslims and the Hindus are all replete with the teaching of ahimsa.
- By ahimsa, we will be able to save the cow and also to win the friendship of the English.

America

It reflects the greatest credit on the determined minority in America that by sheer force of its moral weight, it was able to carry through the prohibition measure, however short-lived.

Anger

- Fasts could not be undertaken out of anger. Anger was a short madness.
- The hardest heart and the grossest ignorance must disappear before the rising sun of suffering without anger and without malice.

Angle

Rectify one angle of a square and the other angles will be automatically right.

Appeasement

- A friendly approach was not one of appeasement. An appeasement was possible between enemies.
- In no case can there be any appeasement at the cost of honour. Real appeasement is to shed all fear and do what is right at any cost.

Armaments

- If the mad race for armaments continues, it is bound to result in a slaughter such as has never occurred in history.
- For India to enter into the race for armaments is to court suicide.

Army

- The power of unarmed non-violence is any day far superior to that of armed force.
- What faith can you place in a general or a soldier?
- One lacks resolution and determination, who says, "I shall keep guard as long as I can?"
- No general ever won a victory by following the principle of 'being vigilant so long as he could.'

Art

- Art to be art must soothe.
- All true art must help the soul to realise its inner self.
- Purity of life is the highest and truest art.
- True art must be evidence of happiness, contentment and purity of the authors.
- True art takes note not merely of form but also of what lies behind.
- The art that is in the machine-made article appeals only to the eye; the art in khadi appeals first to the heart and then to the eye.
- The art of producing good music from cultivated voice can be achieved by many, but the art of producing that music from the harmony of a pure life is achieved very rarely.
- There is a beauty and an art in simplicity which he who runs may see.
- A life of sacrifice is the pinnacle of art and is full of true joy.
- Whatever can be useful to those starving millions is beautiful to my mind.
- I consider writing as a fine art. We kill it by imposing the alphabet on little children and making it the beginning of the learning.
- A semi-starved nation can have neither religion nor art nor organisation.
- Why should I need an artist to explain a work of art to

me? Why should it not speak out to me itself?

- Painters and poets are obliged to exaggerate the proportions of their figures in order to give true perspective. That perspective is never true.
- To a true artist only that face is beautiful which, quite apart from its exterior, shines with the truth within the soul.

Asceticism

By all means drink deep of the fountains that are given to you in the Sermon on the Mount, but then you will have to take sackcloth and ashes.

Astrology

I know nothing of the science of astrology and I consider it to be a science, if it is a science, of doubtful value, to be severely left alone by those who have any faith in providence.

Atheist

God is conscience. He is even the atheism of the atheist.

Atom Bomb

- The atom bomb brought an empty victory to the allied armies but it resulted for the time being in destroying the soul of Japan.
- So far as I can see, the atom bomb has deadened the finest feeling that has sustained mankind for ages.

Autocracy

Mobocracy is autocracy multiplied a million times.

Banker

Even as a banker cannot run a bank if he has nothing in his chest, so can a general not lead in battle if he has no soldiers on whom he can rely implicitly.

Basic education

- Basic education links the children, whether of the cities or villages, to all that is best and lasting in India.
- The object of basic education is the physical, intellectual and moral development of children through the medium of a handicraft.

Beast

Every species, human and sub-human, has some distinguishing mark, so that you can tell a person from a beast or a dog from a cow.

Beauty

- The beauty of poetry is that the creation transcends the poet.
- When I admire the wonder of a sunset or the beauty of the moon, my soul expands in the worship of the creator.
- All truths, not merely ideas, but truthful faces, truthful pictures or songs, are highly beautiful.
- People generally fail to see beauty in truth; the ordinary man runs away from it and becomes blind to the beauty in it.
- Truth is the first thing to be sought for, and beauty and goodness will then be added unto you.

Bhagavadgita (Gita)

- The Gita is not for those who have no faith.
- In the Gita, continuous concentration on God is the king of sacrifices.
- The Gita distinguishes between the powers of light and darkness and demonstrates their incompatibility.
- The Gita is not an aphoristic work; it is a great religious poem.
- Salvation of the Gita is perfect peace.
- A literal interpretation of the Gita lands one in a sea of contradictions.

- The renunciation of the Gita is the acid test of faith.
- The sanyasa of the Gita is all work and yet no work.
- The sanyasa of the Gita will not tolerate complete cessation of activity.
- Devotion required by the Gita is no soft-hearted effusiveness.
- The Bible is as much a book of religion with me as the Gita and the Quran.
- Self-realisation is the object of the Gita, as it is of all scriptures.
- The object of the Gita appears to me to be that of showing the most excellent way to attain self-realisation.
- The message of the Gita is to be found in the second chapter of the Gita where Lord Krishna speaks of the balanced state of mind, of mental equipoise.
- Time is wealth and the Gita says the Great Annihilator annihilates those who waste time.
- According to the letter of the Gita, it is possible to say that warfare is consistent with renunciation of fruit.
- The path of bhakti, karma and love as expounded in the Gita leaves no room for the despising of man by man.
- I have felt that the Gita teaches us that what cannot be followed out in day-to-day practice cannot be called religion.
- My Gita tells me that evil can never result from a good action.
- The Gita is not only my Bible and my Quran; it is more than that. It is my mother.
- I find a solace in the Bhagavadgita and the Upanishads that I miss even in the Sermon on the Mount.
- The Gita has become for me the key to the scriptures of the world.
- Let the Gita be to you a mine of diamonds as it has been to me; let it be your constant guide and friend on life's way.

- The object of the Gita appears to me to be that of showing the most excellent way to attain self-realisation.
- My life has been full of external tragedies and they have not left any visible effect on me; I owe it to the teaching of the Bhagavadgita.
- In the characteristics of the perfected man of the Gita, I do not see any to correspond to physical warfare.
- I still somehow or other fancy that any philosophy represents the true meaning of the teaching of the Gita.
- In order that knowledge may not run riot, the author of the Gita has insisted on devotion accompanying it and has given it the first place.
- The Krishna of the Gita is perfection and right knowledge personified, but the picture is imaginary.
- A devotee of Rama may be said to be the same as the steadfast one of the Gita.
- The seeker is at liberty to extract from this treasure any meaning he likes, so as to enable him to enforce in his life the central teaching.
- To one who reads the spirit of the Gita, it teaches the secret of non-violence, the secret of realising self through the physical body.
- What the Sermon on the Mount describes in a graphic manner, the Bhagavadgita reduces to a scientific formula.
- To those who are ignorant of non-violence, the Gita does not teach any lesson, which is full of despair.
- The Gita is my mother. I lost my earthly mother who gave me birth long ago. But this eternal mother has completely filled her place by my side ever since. She has never changed; she has never failed me. Whenever I am in difficulty or distress, I seek refuge in her bosom.

Birth

- Birth and death are no two different states, but they are different aspects of the same state.
- The whole world is in the throes of new birth. Anything

done for a temporary gain would be tantamount to an abortion.

Birth control

Self-control is the surest and the only method of regulating the birth-rate. Birth control by contraceptives is race suicide.

Blame

Blaming the wolf would not help the sheep much. The sheep must learn not to fall into the clutches of the wolf.

Bone

Every bone picked up is valuable raw material from which useful articles can be made or which can be crushed into rich manure.

Boycott

- Boycott brought about anyhow of British cloth cannot yield the same results as such boycott brought about by hand spinning and khaddar.
- So long as we have to rely on the pins and the needles, figurative and literal, we cannot bring about a complete boycott of foreign goods.
- I boycott foreign goods, not foreign ability.
- We are aware that the business of Swaraj will thrive only if the boycott of foreign cloth is successful.
- If the people resolve and carry out this programme of boycott and swadeshi, they would not have to wait for Swaraj even for a year.

Brahmins (Brahminism)

- The Brahmins are the finest flowers of Hinduism and humanity. I will do nothing to wither them.
- Brahmins are born, not so Brahminism. It is a quality open to be cultivated by the lowliest or the lowest among us.

- A true Brahmin should be the very image of humility and not be proud of his knowledge or wisdom.
- A Brahmin was hardly worth the name, if he did not have the courage of his convictions.
- The Brahmin's duty is to look after the sanitation of the soul; the sweeper's that of the body of the society.
- Where is the real Brahmin today, content with a bare living and giving all his time to study and teaching?
- I have the highest reverence for Brahminism under which a class has been set apart from generation to generation for the exclusive pursuit of divine knowledge and consigned to voluntary poverty.
- I would not have the non-Brahmins to rise on the ruin of the Brahmins.
- Swear all you are worth, if you like, against Brahmins, but never against Brahminism.
- The ideal *bhangi* of my conception would be a Brahmin par excellence, possibly even excel him.

Brave (Bravery)

- Bravery is not man's monopoly.
- Bravery is not a quality of the body, it is of the soul.
- Non-violence is the summit of bravery.
- Bravery on the battlefield is impossible for us. Bravery of the soul still remains open to us.
- I see neither bravery nor sacrifice in destroying life or property for offence or defence.
- Mere brave speech without action is letting off useless steam.
- True *paurush,* true bravery, consists in driving out the brute in us.
- Unexplained bravery, born of non-violence, coupled with strict honesty shown by a fair number of Muslims, was sure to infect the whole of India.
- The art of dying bravely and with honour does not need

any special training, save a living faith in God.

- Active non-violence of the brave puts to flight thieves, dacoits, murders, and prepares an army of volunteers ready to sacrifice themselves in quelling riots, in extinguishing fires and feuds and so on.
- Non-violence is not a weapon of the weak. It is a weapon of the strongest and the bravest.
- There can be no friendship between cowards, and brave men.
- The man or the woman who can display this non-violence of the brave can easily stand against an external invasion.
- Those who are truthful, non-violent and brave do not cease to be so because of the stupidity of their leaders.
- The history of the world is full of instances of men who rose to leadership by sheer force of self-confidence, bravery and tenacity.
- A straight fight in an equal battle takes some bravery, but braver is he who knowing that he would have to sacrifice ninety-five as against five of the enemy, faces death.
- Far better than emasculation would be bravery of those who use physical force.

Brother (Brotherhood)

- All the great religions of the world inculcate the equality and brotherhood of mankind and the virtue of tolerance.
- I want to realise brotherhood or identity not merely with the being called human. But I want to realise identity for the purpose of weaning him from the evil habit.
- A teetotaller would regard it as his duty to associate with his drunkard brother for the purpose of weaning him from the evil habit.
- The khadi spirit means fellow feeling with every human being on earth.
- I have never in my life regarded anyone as my servant, but as a brother or a sister.

Brute (Brute Force)

- Unrestricted individualism is the law of the beast of the jungle.
- The only thing that separates us from the brute, with which we have so much in common, is the capacity to distinguish between right and wrong.
- The spirit lies dormant in the brute, and he knows no law but that of physical might.
- We are no better than the brutes until we have purged ourselves of the sins we have committed against our weaker brethren.
- 'Tit for tat' is the law of the brute or an unregenerate man.
- To answer brutality with brutality is to admit one's moral and intellectual bankruptcy.
- Human nature will only find itself when it fully realises that to be human it has to cease to be beastly or brutal.
- The Germans were defeated not because they were necessarily in the wrong, but because the allied powers were found to possess greater brute strength.
- Brute is the only test the west has hitherto recognised.

Buddha (Buddhism)

- Buddha never rejected Hinduism, but he broadened its base. He gave it a new life and a new interpretation.
- Buddha renounced every worldly happiness because he wanted to share it with the whole world, which was to be had by men who sacrificed and suffered in the search for truth.
- Buddha emphasised and re-declared the eternal and unalterable existence of the moral government of this universe. He unhesitatingly said that the law was God himself.
- For Asia to be not for Asia but the whole world, it has to re-learn the message of the Buddha and deliver it to the world.

- I know that Buddhism is to Hinduism what Protestantism is to Roman Catholicism, only in much stronger light, in a much greater degree.
- I do not believe that 'My philosophy' is an indifferent mixture of Tolstoy and Buddha.

- If there was any teacher in the world who insisted upon the inexorable law of cause and effect, it was Gautama, and yet my friends, the Buddhists outside India, would, if they could, avoid the effects of their own acts.
- Buddhism is the long prayer.

Calamity

There is a divine purpose behind every physical calamity.

Capital (Capitalism)

- No doubt, capital is lifeless, but not the capitalists who are amenable to conversion.
- I do not regard capital to be enemy of labour.
- I am convinced that the capitalist, if he follows the Samurai of Japan, has nothing really to lose and everything to gain.
- I can no more tolerate the yoke of Bolshevism as by Mr. M.N. Roy (radical humanist) than of capitalism.
- What the two hands of the labourer could achieve, the capitalist would never get with all his gold and silver.
- Labour, because it chose to remain unintelligent, either became subservient or insolently believed in damaging the capitalist's goods and machinery or even in killing the capitalists.

Castles in the air

A cave-dweller can build castles in the air, whereas a dweller in a palace like Janak has no castles to build.

Cattle

The half-starved condition of the majority of our cattle is a disgrace to us.

Celibacy

- Celibacy is a great help in as much as it enables one to lead a life of full surrender to God.
- What is brahmacharya? It is the way of life, which leads us to Brahma (God).
- Brahmacharya means control of the senses in thought, word and deed.
- Grihasthashrama is the fair fruit of brahmacharya in life for a number of years.

Changeless

To me I seem to be constantly growing. I must respond to varying conditions, yet remain changeless within.

Character

- Character alone will have real effect on masses.
- Your character must be above suspicion and you must be truthful and self-controlled.
- What will tell in the end will be character and not a knowledge of letters.
- A language is an exact reflection of the character and growth of its speakers.
- Men of stainless character and self-purification will easily inspire confidence and automatically purify the atmosphere around them.
- Sorrow and suffering make for character if they are voluntarily borne, but not if they are imposed.
- A dissolute character is more dissolute in thought than in deed, and the same is true of violence.
- If you have no character to lose, people will have no faith in you.
- The real property that a parent can transmit to all children equally is his or her character and educational facilities.

- A vow imparts stability, ballast and firmness to one's character.
- If you will express the requisite purity of character in action, you cannot do it better than through the spinning wheel.
- All your scholarship, all your study of Shakespeare and Wordsworth would be vain if, at the same time, you do not build your character and attain mastery over your thoughts and actions.
- In the times to come the people will not judge us by the creed we profess or the label we wear or the slogans we shout but by our work, industry, sacrifice, honesty and purity of character.
- Whatever may be the pros and cons of going to the public theatre, it is a patent fact that it has undermined the morals and ruined the character of many a youth in the country.

Charkha (Spinning Wheel)

- The Charkha is an instrument of service.
- The Charkha in the hands of a poor widow brings a paltry price to her, in the hands of Jawaharlal Nehru, it is an instrument of India's freedom.
- The Charkha is an outward symbol of truth and non-violence.
- The Charkha is intended to realise the essential and living oneness of interest among India's myriads.
- The Charkha is the symbol of non-violence on which all life, if it is to be real life, must be based.
- The Charkha is the symbol of sacrifice, and sacrifice is essential for the establishment of the image of the deity.
- The Charkha supplemented the agriculture of the villages and gave it dignity.
- Seek first the Charkha and its concomitants and everything else will be added unto you.
- The Charkha, which is the embodiment of willing obedience and calm persistence, must therefore, succeed before there is civil disobedience.

- Unless the Charkha adds to your ahimsa and makes you stronger every day, your Gandhism is of little avail.
- The turning of the Charkha in a lifeless way will be like the turning of the beads of the rosary with a wandering mind turned away from God.
- I believe that the yarn we spin is capable of mending the broken warp and woof of our life.
- I claim that in losing the spinning wheel we lost our left lung.
- I crave to die with my hand at the spinning wheel.
- I have called spinning the yagya of this age of India.
- If Gandhism means simply machanically turning the spinning wheel, it deserves to be destroyed.
- I have pinned my faith to the spinning wheel, on it; I believe, the salvation of this country depends.
- In my dream, in my sleep, while eating, I think of the spinning wheel. The spinning wheel is my sword. To me it is the symbol of India's liberty.
- My heart is drawn backwards and forwards between spinning wheel and books.
- For every minute that I spin, there is in me the consciousness that I am adding to the nation's wealth.
- The spinning wheel and the spinning wheel alone will solve, if anything will solve, the problem of the deepening poverty of India.
- The spinning wheel means national consciousness and a contribution by every individual to a definite constructive national work.
- The spinning wheel is a symbol of non-violence to me.
- He who spins before the poor, inviting them to do likewise, serves God as no one else does.
- I would like to assure those who would serve Daridanarayana that there is music, art, economy and joy in the spinning wheel.
- The spinning wheel is not meant to oust a single man or woman from his or her occupation.

- The spinning wheel is as much a necessity of Indian life as air and water.
- The spinning wheel is the thing when all must turn in the Indian clime for the transition stage at any rate and the vast majority must for all time.
- The spinning wheel is itself an exquisite piece of machinery. My head daily bows in reverence to its unknown inventor.
- The spinning wheel for us is the foundation for all public corporate life.
- The spinning wheel is the auspicious symbol of sharir yagya i.e. body labour.
- There is no better way of industrialising the villages of India than the spinning wheel.
- If you will express the requisite purity of character in action, you cannot do it better than through the spinning wheel.
- Every woman will tell the curious that with the disappearance of the spinning wheel vanished India's happiness and prosperity.
- There is no 'playing with truth' in the Charkha programme, for satyagraha is not predominently civil disobedience but a quiet and irresistible pursuit of truth.
- The socialism that India can assimilate is the socialism of the spinning wheel.
- The study of Indian economics is the study of the spinning wheel.
- The yagya of our age and for us is the spinning wheel.
- The foundation of service and your real training lie in spinning khaddar.
- The restoration of spinning to its central place in India's peaceful campaign for deliverance from the imperial yoke gives her women a special status.
- Without proper, careful organisation of the spinning wheel and khaddar, there is absolutely no civil disobedience.

- There is a vital connection between satyagraha and Charkha, and the more I find that belief challenged, the more I am confirmed in it.
- The music of the spinning wheel will be as balm to your soul.
- Every widow I have met has recognised in the wheel a dear forgotten friend.
- It was our love of foreign cloth that ousted the wheel from its position of dignity.
- When the wheel was accepted as part of the national flag, it was surely implied that the spinning wheel would hum in every household.
- Hand-spinning is designed to put millions of rupees in the hands of the poor villagers.
- If hand-spinning is an effective method of making India self-supporting, it must be made part of the franchise.
- My swaraj takes note of bhangis, dublas and the weakest of the weak, and except the spinning wheel I know no other thing which befriends all these.
- A plea for the spinning wheel is a plea for recognising the dignity of labour.
- Hunger is the argument that is driving India to the spinning wheel.
- India as a nation can live and die only for the spinning wheel.
- Just as there are signs by which you can recognise violence with the naked eye, so is the spinning wheel to me a decisive sign of non-violence.
- Nothing can so quickly put the masses on their legs as the spinning wheel and all its means.
- Restore the spinning wheel to its place and you will solve the problem of poverty.
- The cause of the spinning wheel is too great and too good to have to rest on mere hero-worship.
- If poet Rabindranath Tagore spins for half an hour daily, his poetry would gain in richness.
- If we are true servants of the masses, we would take pride

in spinning for their sake.

- An hour spent in spinning should be an hour of self-development for the spinner.
- There is no yagya (sacrifice) greater than spinning calculated to bring peace to the troubled spirit, to soothe the distracted student's mind, to spiritualize his life.

Chastity

- Chastity is one of the greatest disciplines without which the mind cannot attain requisite firmness.
- Chastity is not a hothouse growth.

Children

- Children wrapped up in cotton wool are not always proof against all temptation of contamination.
- Our children should not be so taught as to despise labour.
- Basic education links the children, whether of the cities or villages, to all that is best and lasting in India.
- The law of love could be best understood and learnt through little children.
- The greatest lessons in life, if we would but stoop and humble ourselves, we should learn not from the grown-up learned men, but from the so-called ignorant children.
- Pestilence, wars and famines are cursed antidotes against cursed list, which is responsible for unwanted children.

Christ (Christianity)

- Jesus was the most active resister known perhaps to history. His was non-violence par excellence.
- Once Jesus had blazed the trail, his twelve disciples could carry on his mission without his presence.
- Jesus never uttered a loftier or a grandeur truth than when he said that wisdom cometh out of the mouths of the babes.
- Jesus, to me, is a great world teacher among others.
- The message of Jesus has proved ineffective because the

environment was unready to receive it.

- Christianity in India is inextricably mixed up for the last hundred and fifty years with the British rule.
- It is a first class human tragedy that people of the earth who claim to believe in the message of Jesus, whom they describe as the Prince of Peace, show little of that belief in actual practice.
- If I had to face only the Sermon on the Mount and my own interpretation of it, I should not hesitate to say, "Oh yes, I am a Christian."
- I do not accept the orthodox teaching that Jesus was or is God incarnate in the accepted sense or that He was or is the only son of God.
- I love Christianity, Islam and many other faiths through Hinduism.
- Christianity and Islam are but echoes of Hinduism
- The scriptures of Christians, Muslims and Hindus are all replete with the teaching of ahimsa.
- The Allah of Islam is the same as the God of Christians and the Ishwar of Hindus.

Citizenship

- Education in the understanding of citizenship is a short-term affair if we are honest and earnest.
- The emphasis laid on the principle of spending every minute of one's life usefully is the best education for citizenship, and incidentally, it makes basic education self-sufficient.

Civil Disobedience

- Civil disobedience is the assertion of a right which law should give but which it denies.
- Civil disobedience can never be in general terms, such as for independence.
- Civil disobedience is an ostimulation for the fighters and a challenge to the opponent, in the present instance—authority.

- Civil disobedience presupposes willing obedience of our self-imposed rules, and without it civil obedience would be a cruel joke.
- Civil disobedience is not only the natural right of a people, especially when they have no effective voice in their own Government, but that it is also a substitute for violence or armed rebellion.
- Civil disobedience is the inherent right of a citizen.
- Civil disobedience becomes a sacred duty when the state has become lawless or corrupt.
- Civil disobedience can only lead to strength and purity.
- Civil disobedience is a preparation for mute suffering.
- Civil disobedience means capacity for ultimate suffering, without the intoxicating excitement of killing.
- Civil disobedience does not admit of any violence or countenancing of violence, directly or indirectly.
- Civil disobedience and excitement and intoxication go ill together.
- Individual civil disobedience was everybody's inherent right, like the right of self-defence in normal life.
- Mass civil obedience was for the attainment of independence.
- Mass civil disobedience is like an earthquake, a sort of general upheaval on the political plane.
- Complete civil disobedience is a state of peaceful rebellion, a refusal to obey every single state-made law.
- Aggressive civil disobedience should be confirmed to a vindication of the right of free speech and free association.
- In placing civil disobedience before constructive work, I was wrong and I did not profit by the Himalayan blunder that I had committed.
- Disobedience, to be civil, has to be open and non-violent.
- Disobedience, to be civil, implies discipline, thought, care and attention.
- Disobedience that is wholly civil should never provoke retaliation.

- Before civil disobedience can be practised on a vast scale, people must learn the art of civil or voluntary obedience.
- Active non-violence is necessary for those who will offer civil disobedience but the will and proper training is enough for the people to co-operate with those who are chosen for civil disobedience.
- Non-co-operation and civil disobedience are but different branches of the same tree, called satyagraha.
- The Charkha, which is the embodiment of willing obedience and calm persistence, must, therefore, succeed before there is civil disobedience.
- Satyagraha does not begin and end with civil disobedience.
- Satyagraha of which civil resistance is but a part is to me the universal law of life.
- The liberty of the press is a dear privilege apart from the advisability or otherwise of civil disobedience.
- When neglect of the call means a denial of God, civil disobedience becomes a peremptory duty.
- Indeed a civil resister offers resistance only when peace becomes impossible.
- Ours is a civil fight, and imprisonment as a civil prisoner has got to be earned by the strict observance of the programme.
- If people are truly non-violent, they must also realise that civil disobedience is an impossibility till the preliminary work of construction is done.
- For Satyagraha and its offshoots, non-co-operation and civil resistance are nothing but new names for the law of suffering.
- The privilege of resisting or disobeying a particular law or order accrues only to him who gives willing and unswerving obedience to the laws laid down for him.

Civilisation

- Civilisation has come and gone, and in spite of our

vaunted progress, I am tempted to ask again and again, "To what purpose?"

- Civilisation is not an incurable disease, but it should never be forgotten that the English people are at present afflicted by it.
- Civilisation is that mode of conduct which paints out to man the path of duty.
- Civilisation, in the real sense of the term, consists not in the multiplication but in the deliberate and voluntary reduction of wants.
- This civilisation is such that one has only to be patient and it will be self-destroyed.
- Is a civilisation worth the name which requires for its existence the very doubtful prop of a social legislation and a lynch law?
- Modern civilisation has taught us to convert night into day and golden silence into brazen and noise.
- The truest test of civilisation, culture and dignity is character and not clothing.
- Further march of civilisation seems to employ increasing domination of man over beast, together with a growing humane method of using them.
- The British Government in India constitutes a struggle between the modern civilisation, which is the kingdom of Satan, and the ancient civilisation, which is the kingdom of God.
- I want co-operation between nations for the salvaging of civilisation, but co-operation presupposes free nations worthy of co-operation.
- Civilisation based on non-violence must be different from that organised for violence.

Civil resistance

- In mass civil resistance, leadership is essential; in individual civil resistance, every resister is his own leader.

- The field of research in civil resistance is necessarily limited, as the occasions for civil resistance in a man's life are not to be frequent.

Cleanliness

- It does not require money to be neat, clean and dignified.
- Members of a family will keep their house clean, but they will not be interested in the neighbour's.

Coercion

- Coercion cannot but result in chaos in the end.
- The man who uses coercion is guilty of deliberate violence. Coercion is inhuman.
- Since Satyagraha is a method of conversion and conviction, it seeks never to use the slightest coercion.
- My method is conversion, not coercion; it is self-suffering, not the suffering of the tyrant.

Communism (Bolshevism)

- Communism, as I have understood it, is a natural corollary of socialism.
- The socialistic conception of the West was born in an environment reeking with violence.
- Our socialism or communism should be based on non-violence and on harmonious co-operation of labour and capital, landlord and tenant.
- I claim to be a foremost communist although I make use of cars and other facilities offered to me by the rich.

Compromise

The essential condition of a compromise is that there should be nothing humiliating and nothing panicky about it.

Compulsion

Compulsion means submission by protestors to the thing

they oppose under pain of being fined or imprisoned.

Concentration

Counting beads with the name of Allah or Ishwar on one's lips whilst the mind wanders in all directions is worse than useless.

Conduct

- The safest rule of conduct is to claim kinship when we want to do service, and not to insist on kinship when we want to assert a right.
- I am painfully aware of the fact that conduct everywhere falls far short of relief.

Confession

- Confession of error is like a broom that sweeps away the dirt and leaves the surfaces cleaner than before.
- Prayer is a confession of one's unworthiness and weakness.
- I feel stronger for my confession. And the cause must prosper for the retracing.
- Indeed, the errors and my prompt confessions have made me surer of my insight into the implications of truth and ahimsa.

Conscience

- Conscience can reside only in delicately tuned breast.
- For me the voice of God, of conscience, of truth, or the inner voice of 'the still small voice' mean one and the same thing.

Constructive programme

Remember that no political programme can stand without the constructive programme.

Contentment

I would like people to compete with me in my contentment. It is the richest treasure I won.

Control

If my non-violence is to be contagious and infectious, I must acquire greater control over my thoughts.

Conversion

- Conversion is a matter of heart and reason. An appeal to heart and reason can only be made through conduct.
- Conversion without a clean heart is a denial of God and Religion.
- Conversion without cleanliness of heart can only be a matter of sorrow, not joy, to a godly person.
- Surely conversion is a matter between man and his maker who alone knows His creatures' hearts.
- I believe in conversion of mankind, not its destruction.

Co-operation

- I was a co-operator too in the sense that I non-cooperated for co-operation, and even then I said that if I could carry the country forward by co-operation I should co-operate.
- My non-co-operation is a token of my earnest longing for real heart co-operation in the place of co-operation falsely so-called.
- Non-cooperation with evil is as much a duty as co-operation with good.
- At times, non-cooperation becomes as much a duty as co-operation.
- Non-violent action without the co-operation of the heart and the head cannot produce the intended result.
- The nation's non-co-operation is an invitation to the Government to co-operate with it in its own terms, as it is every nation's right and every good government's duty.
- A drop torn from the ocean perishes without doing any good.

Copyright

- Copyright is not a natural thing. It is a modern institution, perhaps desirable to a certain extent.
- Writings in the journals which I have the privilege of editing must be common property.

Correction

Error ceases to be error when it is corrected.

Corruption

Corruption and hypocrisy ought not to be inevitable products of democracy, as they undoubtedly are today.

Cottage industry

The cottage industry of India had to perish in order that Lancashire might flourish.

Courage

- Human dignity demands the courage to defend oneself.
- Ahimsa calls for the strength and courage to suffer without retaliation, to receive blows without returning any.

Cow

- The cow to me is a Sermon on pity.
- The cow is the purest type of sub-human life.
- Mother cow is as useful when dead as when she is alive.
- Mother cow expects from us nothing but grass and grain.
- Mother cow is in many ways better than the mother who gave us birth.
- Man through the cow is enjoined to realise his identity with all that lives.
- Cow-protection is the gift of Hinduism to the world.
- Cow-protection to me is one of the most wonderful phenomena in the human evolution.

- We cry for cow-protection in the name of religion, but we refuse protection to the human cow in the shape of the girl widow.
- Cow-protection can only be secured by cultivating universal friendliness, i.e. ahimsa.
- Cow-protection means protection of the weak, the helpless, the dumb and the deaf.
- Cow-protection to me is protection more than mere protection of the cow.
- The central fact of Hinduism is cow protection.
- Cow preservation is an article of faith in Hinduism.
- The only way Hindus can convert the whole world to cow protection is by giving an object lesson in cow-protection and all it means.
- My religion teaches me that I should by my personal conduct instill into the minds of those who might hold different views the conviction that cow-killing is a sin.
- By ahimsa we will be able to save the cow and also win the friendship of the English.
- When I see a cow, I know it is not an animal to eat; it is a poem of pity for me and I worship it, and I shall defend its worship against the whole world.
- Cow-slaughter and man-slaughter are in my opinion the two sides of the same coin.
- Cow-slaughter can never be stopped by law.
- Nowhere in the world you find such skeletons of cows and bullocks as you do in our cow-worshipping India.

Coward (Cowardice)

- Cowardice was incompatible with divine wisdom.
- Cowardice is no sign of belief in God.
- Cowardice, whether philosophical or otherwise, abhors.
- Far better than cowardice is to kill or be killed in battle.
- Could there be a greater proof of our cowardice than fighting amongst ourselves?
- No police or military in the world can protect people who are cowards.

- There can be no friendship between cowards or cowards and brave men.
- It was the cowards who died many times before their death.
- It is better to be charged with cowardice and weakness than to be guilty of denial of our oath and sin against God.
- Non-violence is the virtue of the manly.
- Non-violence and cowardice go ill together.
- Between violence and cowardly fight, I can only prefer violence to cowardice.
- Non-violence should never be used as a shield for cowardice. It was a weapon of the brave.
- To change one's religion under the threat of force was no conversion, but rather cowardice.
- To retaliate against the relatives of the co-religionists of the wrongdoer is a cowardly act.
- I can no more preach non-violence to a cowardly man than I can tempt a blind man to enjoy healthy scenes.
- Far better than emasculation would be the bravery of those who use physical force. Far better than cowardice would be meeting one's death fighting in battle.
- I would rather have India resort to arms in order to defend her honour than she should in a cowardly manner become or remain a helpless witness to her own dishonour.
- The truth is that cowardice itself is violence of a subtle kind and, therefore, dangerous type and far more difficult to eradicate than the habit of physical violence.
- Where there is only a choice between cowardice and violence, I would advise violence.
- For thousands to go to death for a few hundred is no bravery. It is worse than cowardice. It is unworthy of nationalism, of any religion.

Creator

Religion is the tie that binds one to one's creator, and whilst the body perishes, as it has to, religion persists even after death.

Crime

Crime is like a disease, like any other malady, and is a product of the prevalent social system.

Criticism

- Healthy, well-informed, balanced criticism is the ozone of public life.
- Volunteers should regard criticism as the food on which they live.
- Intolerance of criticism even of what one may prize as dear as life itself is not conducive to the growth of public corporate life.
- Surely, Islam has nothing to fear from criticism even if it is unreasonable.

Cruel

God cannot be as cruel and unjust as to make the distinctions of high and low between man and man, and woman and woman.

Culture

- A nation's culture resides in the hearts and in the souls of its people.
- Mutual courtesy and respect was the foundation of culture.
- No culture can live if it attempts to be exclusive.
- It is my firm opinion that no culture has treasures as rich as ours has.
- The truest test of civilisation, culture and dignity is character and not clothing.
- Every ideal in India is a synthesis of the different cultures that have come to stay in India, that have influenced Indian life, and that, in their turn, have themselves been

influenced by the spirit of the soil.

- I claim to represent all the cultures, for my religion, whatever it may be called, demands the fulfillment of all the cultures.
- My religion forbids me to belittle or disregard other cultures, as it insists under pain of civil suicide upon imbibing and living my own.

Daridranarayana

- Daridranarayana is insatiable and there is room enough in his belly for all the money and the ornaments you can give.
- The real Daridranarayana even I have not seen, but know only through my imagination.
- I would like to assure those who would serve Daridranarayana that there is music, art, economy and joy in the spinning wheel.
- Of all the myriad of God, Daridranarayana is the most sacred, in as much as it represents the untold millions of poor people as distinguished from the few rich people.
- It is my great misfortune that I have to measure your love by the money gifts you give for Daridranarayana.

Death

- Death is at any time blessed, but it is twice blessed for a warrior who dies for his cause, that is, truth.
- S of the friends. He delivers us from agony.
- Death on the battlefield is welcome to a soldier.
- To die in the act of killing is in essence to die defeated.
- Birth and death are not two different states, but they are different aspects of the same state.
- It is as clear to me as daylight that life and death are but phases of the same thing, the reverse and obverse of the same coin.
- A courageous man prefers death to the surrender of self-respect.

- Life becomes livable only to the extent that death is treated as a friend, never as an enemy.
- If love was not the law of life, life would not have persisted in the midst of death.
- True ahimsa should wear a smile even on a deathbed brought about by an assailant. It is only with that ahimsa that we can define our opponents and win their love.
- It was the cowards who died many times before their death.
- If we weep for all the deaths in our country, the tears in our eyes would never dry.
- No amount of casuistry can defend the penalty of stoning to death in any event or that of death, whether by stoning or otherwise, for apostasy.
- Where death without resistance or death after resistance is the olny way, neither party should think of resorting to law-counts or help from the government.
- What is imprisonment to the man who is fearless of death itself?
- I came alone in this world; I have walked alone in the valley of the shadow of death, and I shall quit alone when the time comes.
- I can see that in the midst of death life persists; in the midst of untruth truth persists; in the midst of darkness light persists. Hence I gather that God is Life, Truth and Light. He is love. He is the supreme good.
- You may pluck out my eyes but that cannot kill me. You may chop off my nose, but that will not kill me. But blast my belief in God, and I am dead.
- It is much more difficult to live for non-violence than to die for it.
- History is replete with instances of men who by dying with courage and compassion on their lips converted the hearts of their violent opponents.
- Slow and inglorious self-imposed starvation among the starving masses is every time more heroic than the death of the scaffold under false exaltation.

Debt

- In the billiard room and on the tennis-court, think of the big debt that is being piled against you from day-to-day.
- What God may have enabled me to do is but a repayment of debt, and he who repays a debt-deserves no praise.

Deception

Terrorism and deception are weapons, not of the strong but of the weak.

Defeat

- Heroes are made in the hour of defeat. Success is, therefore, well described as a series of glorious defeats.
- Never own defeat in a sacred cause and make up your minds henceforth that you will be pure and that you will find response from God.
- Defeat has no place in the dictionary of non-violence.

Defence

- It is the Maginot line (for defence of France constructed by France on her frontier) that has made the Siegfried Line (for defence of Germany constructed by Germany on her frontier) necessary and vice versa.
- Whatever one or many think I must declare my faith that it is better for India to discard violence altogther even for defending her borders.

Democracy

- Democracy necessarily means a conflict of will and ideas, involving sometimes a war to the knife between different ideas.
- Democracy can only represent the average, if not less than the average.
- The very essence of democracy is that every person

represents all the varied interests, which compose the nation.

- Democracy comes naturally to him who is habituated normally to yield willing obedience to all laws, human or divine.
- Democracy demands patient instruction on it before legislation.
- Democracy, disciplined and enlightened, is the finest thing in the world.
- Democracy and dependence on the military and police are incompatible.
- Democracy is a great institution and, therefore, it is liable to be greatly abused.
- Democracy is an impossible thing until the power is shared by all, but let not democracy degenerate into mobocracy.
- Democracy is not a state in which people act like sheep.
- Democracy and violence go ill together.
- Evolution of democracy is not possible if we are not prepared to hear the other side.
- The spirit of democracy cannot be imposed from without. It has to come from within.
- In the days of democracy there is no such thing as active loyalty to a person. You are, therefore, loyal or disloyal to institutions.
- Democracy will break under the strain of apron strings. It can exist only on trust.
- Islam was nothing if it did not spell complete democracy.
- My notion of democracy is that under it the weakest should have the same opportunity as the strongest.
- To safeguard democracy the people must have a keen sense of independence, self-respect and their oneness.
- What is really needed to make democracy function is not knowledge of facts, but right education.
- Intolerance, discourtesy and harshness are taboo in all good society, and are surely contrary to the spirit of democracy.

- The line of demarcation between democracy and mobocracy is often thin, but rigid and stronger than unbreakable steel.
- In true democracy every man and woman is taught to think for himself or herself.
- The spirit of democracy cannot be established in the midst of terrorism, whether governmental or popular.
- The spirit of democracy is not a mechanical thing to be adjusted by abolition of forms. It requires change of heart.
- People in a democracy should be satisfied with drawing the government's attention to mistake, if any.
- You have to uphold democracy; democracy and dependence on the military and the police are incompatible.
- Under democracy, individual liberty of opinion and action is jealously guarded.
- No perfect democracy is possible without perfect non-violence at the back of it.
- The only force at the disposal of democracy is that of public opinion.
- True democracy is not inconsistent with a few persons representing the spirit, the hope and the aspirations of those whom they claim to represent.
- A born democrat is a born disciplinarian.
- A democrat must be utterly selfless. He must think and dream not in terms of self or of party, but only of democracy.
- The true democrat is he who with purely non-violent means defends his liberty and, therefore, his country's, and ultimately that of the whole of mankind.
- A democratic organisation has to dare to do the right at all costs.
- If fighting for the legislatures meant a sacrifice of truth and non-violence, democracy would not be worth a moment's purpose.

Dependence

No nation being under another nation can accept gifts and kick at the responsibility attaching to those gifts imposed by the conquering nation.

Desire

- By means of a desire for enjoyment we have created and continued to maintain this encumbrance in the shape of the body.
- When there is no desire for fruit, there is also no temptation for untruth or himsa.

Despair

- 'Despair' is a term, which does not occur in my dictionary.
- I shall despair when I am despaired of myself, of God and humanity.

Destiny

- Man is the maker of his own destiny, and I, therefore, ask you to become makers of your own destiny.
- To find truth completely is to realise oneself and one's destiny to become perfect.

Devotee (Devotion)

- Devotion to this truth is the sole justification for our effusiveness.
- Devotion required by the Gita is not soft-hearted effusiveness.
- Without devotion, action and knowledge are cold and dry, and may even become shackles.
- A devotee may use, if he likes, rosaries, forehead marks, make offerings, but these things are not test of his devotion.
- The path of bhakti, karma and love as expounded in the Gita leaves no room for the despising of man by man.
- Knowledge without devotion will be like a misfire.

- Renunciation is the central sun, round which devotion, knowledge and the rest revolve like planets.
- Knowledge and devotion, to be true, have to stand the test of renunciation of the fruits of action.
- One rupee can purchase for us poison or nectar, but knowledge or devotion cannot buy either salvation or bondage.
- In order that knowledge may not run riot, the author of the Gita has insisted on devotion accompanying it and has given it the first place.

Diagnosis

- A correct diagnosis is three-fourths the remedy.
- The truest test of civilisation, culture and dignity is character and not clothing.

Diplomacy

I know no diplomacy save that of truth.

Disarmament

A free India will throw all her weight in favour of world disarmament and She should be prepared to give a lead in this.

Discipline

- True discipline gives enthusiastic obedience to instructions even though they do not satisfy the reason.
- A disciplined army of a few hundred trained men has, times without number, routed countless undisciplined hordes.
- Conscience is the ripe fruit of strictest discipline.
- A student's life has been rightly likened to the life of a sanyasi. He must be the embodiment of simple living and high thinking. He must be discipline incarnate. His pleasure is derived from his studies.
- Unless the discipline is rooted in non-violence, it might

prove a source of infinite mischief.

- For winning swaraj one requires iron discipline.
- A man who would interpret the scriptures must have the spiritual discipline.
- Chastity is one of the greatest disciplines without which the mind cannot attain requisite firmness.
- I have not known of a war gained by a rabble, but I have known of wars gained by disciplined armies.
- Non-co-operation is a measure of discipline and sacrifice, and it demands respect for the opposite views.

Disease

We are like the nurses who may not leave their patients because they are reported to have an incurable disease.

Dishonesty

A businessman who lies to and cheats his simple-minded and ignorant customers cannot hope to be saved.

Distinctions

Labour was a great leveller of all distinctions.

Distruct

It is weakness which breeds fear, and fear breeds distrust.

Divine rights

There is no such thing as the divine right of the kings to rule and the humble duty of the ryots to pay respectful obedience to their masters.

Divinity

- Divine knowledge is not borrowed from books. It has to be realised by oneself.
- The meaning of prayer is that I want to evoke the Divine within me.

- The Divine Radio is always singing; we could only make ourselves ready to listen to it, but it is impossible to listen without silence.
- There is a divine purpose behind every physical calamity.
- My belief in the Hindu scriptures does not require me to accept every word and every verse as divinely inspired.

Doctor

A doctor who uses his talent to pander to the vice of his patient degrades himself and his patient.

Dominion Status

Dominion status is nothing if it does not mean the ability of the dominion in question to stand by itself.

Dream

Close the day with prayer so that you may have a peaceful night - free from dreams and nightmares.

Drink

- Drink makes a man forget himself. He ceases to be a man for the time being. He becomes less than a beast.
- It is wrong and immoral for a nation to supply intoxicating liquor to those who are addicted to drink.

Duty

- Civilisation is that mode of conduct, which points out to man the path of duty.
- A duty religiously performed carries with it several other important consequences.
- A man can give up a right, but he may not give up a duty without being guilty or a grave dereliction.
- Means to be means must always be within our reach, and so ahimsa is our supreme duty.
- Ahimsa is the highest duty. Even if we cannot practise it

in full, we must try to understand its spirit and refrain as far as is humanly possible from violence.

- Performance of duty and observance of morality are convertible terms.
- Out of the performance of duties flow rights, and those that knew and performed their duties came naturally by the rights.
- A pure fast, like duty, is its own reward.
- The true source of rights is duty.
- If leaving duties unperformed we run after rights, they will escape us like a will-o-the-wisp.
- If we all discharge our duties, rights will not be far to seek.
- A wretched parent, who claims obedience from his children, without first doing his duty to them, excites nothing but contempt.
- He who is ever brooding over result often loses in the performance of his duty.
- No people have risen who thought only of rights. Only those did who thought of duties.
- You cannot neglect the nearer duty for the sake of a remote one.
- Violence becomes imperative when an attempt is made to assert rights without any reference to duties.
- In my humble opinion, non-co-operation with evil is as much a duty as is co-operation with good.
- I know, too, that performance of one's duty should be independent of public opinion.
- I know that not only is Swaraj our birthright, but it is our sacred duty to win it.
- No displeasure, even of the dearest friends, can put me off the duty I see clearly in front of me.

Earning

May not men earn their bread by intellectual labour? No. The needs of the body must be supplied by the body.

Earth

The little globe of ours is not a toy of yesterday.

Eating

Eating for the sake of pleasure is a sin like animal indulgence for the sake of it.

Economics

- Economics that hurts the moral well-being of an individual or a nation is immoral and, therefore, sinful.
- That economics is untrue which ignores or disregards moral values.
- The study of Indian Economics is the study of the spinning wheel.
- We can try to analyse economic trends; we can't run against them in a head-on collision.

Education

- An education which does not teach us to discriminate between good and bad, to assimilate the one and eschew the other, is a misnomer.
- Education should be so revolutionised as to answer the wants of the poorest villager, instead of answering those of an imperial exploiter.
- Education in the understanding of citizenship is a short term affair if we are honest and earnest.
- Basic education links the children, whether of the cities or the villages, to all that is best and lasting in India.
- Is not education the art of drawing out full manhood of the children under training?
- Literacy itself is no education.
- Literacy is not the end of education or even the beginning.
- Literacy education should follow the education of the hand—the one gift that visibly distinguishes man from beast.

- Real education has to draw out the best from the boys and girls to be educated.
- True education must correspond to the surrounding circumstances or it is not a healthy growth.
- What is really needed to make democracy function is not knowledge of facts, but right education.
- National education to be truly national must reflect the national condition for the time being.
- The function of *Nayee-Talim* is not to teach an occupation, but through it to develop the whole man.
- I believe that religious education must be the sole concern of religious association.
- By education I mean an all-round drawing out of the best in the child and man - body, mind and spirit.
- By spiritual training I mean education of the heart.
- Experience gained in the schools under my control has taught me that punishment does not purify; if anything, it hardens children.
- I consider writing a fine art. We kill it by imposing the alphabet on little children and making it the beginning of learning.
- I do regard spinning and weaving as the necessary part of any national system of education.
- The aim of university education should be to turn out true servants of the people who will live and die for the country's freedom.
- A balanced intellect presupposes a harmonious growth of body, mind and soul.
- Love requires that true education should be easily accessible to all and should be of use to every villager in his daily life.
- The notion of education through handicrafts rises from the contemplation of truth and love permeating life's activities.
- The fees that you pay do not cover even a fraction of the

amount that is spent on your education from the public exchequer.

- Persistent questioning and healthy inquisitiveness are the first requisite for acquiring learning of any kind.
- If we want to impart education best suited to the needs of the villagers, we should take the *vidyapeeth* to the villages.
- In a democratic scheme, money invested in the promotion of learning gives a tenfold return to the people even as a seed sown in good soil returns a luxuriant crop.
- All education in a country has got to be demonstrably in promotion of the progress of the country in which it is given.
- The canker has so eaten into the society that in many cases the only meaning of education is knowledge of English.
- The emphasis laid on the principle of spending every minute of one's life usefully is the best education for citizenship.

Effort

The pleasure lies in making the effort, not in its fulfillment.

Ego

We are all like water: we have to strive so to rarefy ourselves that all the ego in us perishes and we merge in the infinite to the eternal good of all.

Employment

Khadi will cease to have any value in my eyes if it does not usefully employ the millions.

Enemy

- In the dictionary of satyagraha, there is no enemy.
- No man could look upon another as his enemy unless he first became his own enemy.

Englishman (English language)

- Englishmen must learn to be Brahmins, not banias.
- Civilisation is not an incurable disease, but it should never be forgotten that the English people are at present afflicted by it.
- Non-co-operation is a movement intended to invite Englishmen to co-operate with us on honourable terms or retire from our land.
- Swaraj means a state such that we can maintain our separate existence without the presence of the English.
- However, virile the English language may be, it can never become the language of the masses of India.
- The English language is so elastic that you can find another word to say the same thing.
- If the English educated neglect, as they have done and even now continue, as some do, to be ignorant of their mother tongue, linguistic starvation will abide.
- We, the English educated Indians, often unconsciously make the terrible mistake of thinking that the microscopic minority of the English-speaking Indians is the whole of India.
- I am not anti-English; I am not anti-British; I am not anti-Government, but I am anti-untruth, anti-humbug and anti-injustice.
- I refuse to put the unnecessary strain of learning English upon my sisters for the sake of false pride or questionable social advantage.
- My love of the British is equal to that of my own people.
- My mission is to convert every Indian, every Englishman, and finally the world to non-violence for regulating mutual relations, whether political economic, social or religious.
- My personal religion enables me to serve my countrymen without hurting the English or, for that matter, anybody else.
- My plea is for banishing the English language as a

cultural usurper, as we successfully banished the political rule of the English usurper.

- If any Englishman dedicated his life to securing the freedom of India, resisting tyranny and serving the land, I should welcome that Englishman as an Indian.
- Personally, I crave not for independence, but I long for freedom from the English yoke.
- By patriotism I mean the welfare of the whole people, and if I could secure it at the hands of the English, I should bow down my head to them.
- Through the deliverance of India, I seek to deliver the so-called weaker races of the earth from the crushing heels of western exploitation in which England is the greatest partner.
- To get rid of the infatuation for English is one of the essentials of Swaraj.
- A smattering of English is worse than useless; it is an unnecessary tax on our women.
- Of all the superstitions that affect India, none is as great as that the knowledge of the English language is necessary for imbibing ideas of liberty and developing accuracy to thought.
- We, Hindus and Mohammedans, would have to blame our folly rather than the English, if we allowed them to put us asunder.
- It would be a sad day for India if it has to inherit the English scale and the English tastes so utterly unsuitable to the Indian Government.
- My heart rebels against any foreigner imposing on my country the peace which is here called Pax-Britannica.
- Christianity in India is inextricably mixed up for the last hundred and fifty years of the British rule.
- No matter what the cause was and wherever it was, Indian Government must never requisition the services of British soldiers to deal with civil disturbances.

- There is as much need for a change of heart among the Hindus and Mohamedans as there is among the British, before a proper settlement is arrived at.
- Let us learn from the English rulers the simple fact that the oppressors are blind to the enormity of their own misdeeds.
- Man had the supreme knack of deceiving himself; the Englishman was super most amongst men.
- The British is the top dog and the Indian the underdog in his own country.
- That I want to destroy the British imperialism is another matter, but I want to do so by converting those who are associated with it.
- India is less manly under the British rule than she ever was before.
- The British are weak in numbers; we are weak in spite of our numbers.
- My motto is, "unite now, today if you can; fight if you must. But in every case, avoid British intervention."
- Will Great Britain have an unwilling India dragged into war or a willing ally co-operating with her in the prosecution of a defence of true democracy?
- Boycott brought about anyhow of British cloth cannot yield the same results as such boycott brought about by hand-spinning and khaddar.
- I must fight unto death the unholy attempt to impose British methods and British institutions on India.
- The Indian struggle is not anti-British; it is anti-exploitation, anti-foreign rule, not anti-foreigners.
- The way out of the riots, on the one hand, and the British bayonets on the other, is frank acceptance of non-violence.
- What senseless violence does is to prolong the lease of life of the British or foreign rule.
- Our non-violence vis-a-vis the British Government has been the non-violence of the weak.

- I believe in the capacity of India to offer non-violent battle to the English rulers.

- The builders of the British Indian empire have patiently built its four pillars—the European interests, the army, the Indian princes and the communal divisions.
- The collector of revenue and the policeman are the only symbols by which millions in India's villages know British rule.
- It was not through democratic methods that Britain bagged India.
- For my own part, I do not want the freedom of India if it means extinction of English or the disappearance of Englishman.
- It is derogatory to the dignity of mankind; it is derogatory to the dignity of India, to entertain for one single moment hatred towards Englishmen.
- If you must kill English officials, why not kill me instead?
- I am just not thinking of India's deliverance. It will come, but will it be worth if England and France fall, or if they come out victorious over Germany ruined and humbled?
- I claim to have been a lifelong and wholly disinterested friend of the British people.
- My attitude towards the British is one of utter friendliness and respect.
- I may fight the British ruler, but I do not hate the English or the English language. In fact, I appreciate their literary treasures.

Equality

- Equality of sexes does not mean equality of occupations.
- Economic equality of my conception does not mean that everyone will literally have the same amount.
- The real meaning of economic equality is 'to each according to his need'.
- What is equality of rights between a giant and a dwarf?

- Economic equality is the master-key to non-violent Independence.
- The prince and the peasant will not be equalised by cutting off the prince's head.
- No two leaves are alike, and yet there is no antagonism between them or between the branches on which they grow.
- If a single man demanded as much as a man with a wife and four children, that would be a violation of the concept of economic equality.
- 'All men are born equal and free' is not Nature's law in the literal sense.
- My idea of society is that while we are born equal, meaning that we have a right to equal opportunity, all have not the same capacity.
- Let no one try to justify the glaring difference between the classes and the masses, the prince and the pauper by saying that the former needs more.
- The real implication of equal distribution is that each man shall have the wherewithal to supply all his natural needs and no more.
- The elephant needs a thousand times more food than the ant but that is not an indication of inequality.
- No man is a true believer unless he desires for his brother that which he desires for himself.
- How can I even secretly harbour the thought that my neighbour's faith is inferior to mine?

Ethics

- Teaching of fundamental ethics is undoubtedly a function of the state.
- By religion I have not in mind fundamental ethics but what goes by the name of denominationalism.
- To me, God is Truth and Love; God is ethics and morality; God is fearlessness.

Euclid

- Euclid's line is one without breadth, but no one has so far been able to draw it and never will.
- If Euclid's print, thought incapable of being drawn by human agency, has an imperishable value, my picture has its own for mankind to live.
- Absolute trusteeship is an abstraction like Euclid's definition of a point and is equally unattainable.

Europe

- Europe is today only nominally Christian. It is really worshipping Mammon.
- European civilisation is no doubt suited for the Europeans, but it will mean ruin for India, if we endeavour to copy it.
- An India prostrate at the feet of Europe can give no hope to humanity.
- A free India will claim to examine every European interest on its merits and that which conflicts with the national interest will go by the board.

Evil

- Not until we have reduced ourselves to nothingness can we conquer the evil in us.
- He who has a living faith in God will not do evil deeds with the name of God on his lips.
- Non-co-operation is a protest against an unwitting and unwilling participation in evil.
- Non-violence does not signify that man must not fight against the enemy, and by enemy is meant the evil which men do, not the human beings themselves.
- Real non-co-operation is no co-operation with evil and not with the evildoer.
- In a strictly scientific sense God is at the bottom of both good and evil.

- Tolerance obviously does not disturb the distinction between right and wrong or good and evil.

Evolution

- Like man, the meaning of great writings suffers evolution.
- The religion of our conception, thus imperfect, is always subject to a process of evolution and re-interpretation.
- My experiments I hold to be infinitely more important than the best equipped Himalayan expeditions.

Exploitation

- The divorce of intellect from body labour has made us perhaps the shortest lived, most resource less and most exploited nation on earth.
- Exploitation and domination of one nation over another can have no place in a world striving to put an end to all war.
- Through the deliverance of India, I seek to deliver the so-called weaker races of the earth from the crushing heels of western exploitation in which England is the greatest partner.

Faith

- Faith becomes lame, when it ventures into matters pertaining to reason.
- A faith gained in strength only when people were willing to lay down their lives for it.
- Faith is like the Himalayas, which cannot possibly change.
- Faith is not a delicate flower, which would wither away under the slightest stormy weather.
- Robust faith in oneself and brave trust of the opponent so called or real, is the best safeguard.
- Exercise of faith will be the safest where there is a clear determination summarily to reject all that is contrary to truth and love.

- A living faith cannot be manufactured by the rule of majority.
- What is faith worth if it is not translated into action?
- If you have faith in the cause and means and in God, the hot sun will be cool for you.
- It is poor faith that needs fair weather for standing firm. That alone is true faith that stands the foulest weather.
- Nothing can be more hurtful to an honourable man than he should be accused of bad faith.
- Faith is not imparted like secular subjects. It is given through the language of the heart.
- Every living faith must have within itself the power of rejuvenation if it is to live.
- Work without faith is like an attempt to reach the bottom of a bottomless pit.
- A man with a grain of faith never loses hope, because he ever believes in the ultimate triumph of truth.
- A man of faith does not bargain or stipulate with God.
- Just as the body cannot exist without blood, so the soul needs the matchless and pure strength of faith.
- Non-violence succeeds only when we have a real living faith in God.
- A satyagrahi should have a living faith in God.
- The Gita is not for those who have no faith.
- I am a seasoned soldier of non-violence, and I have evidence enough to sustain my faith.
- I know nothing of the science of astrology and I consider it to be a science, if it is a science, of doubtful value, to be severely left alone by those who have any faith in Providence.
- It is the faith and perseverance and single-mindedness with which Hitler has perfected his weapons of destruction that commands my admiration.
- God's word is: "He who strives never perishes." I have implicit faith in that promise.

- My effort should never be to undermine another's faith but to make him a better follower of his own faith.
- My faith in non-co-operation is as bright as ever.
- My faith is brightest in the midst of impenetrable darkness.
- My faith runs so very much faster than my reason that I can challenge the whole world and say, "God is, was and ever shall be".
- The only tyrant I accept in this world is the 'still small voice' within.
- My implicit faith in non-violence does mean yielding to minorities when they are really weak.
- Non-violence is the first article of my faith. It is also the last article of my creed.
- Whether one or many may oppose, I must declare my faith that it is better for India to discard violence altogether even for defending her borders.
- With me, the connection between the cosmic phenomena and human behaviour is a living faith that draws me nearer to God, humbles me and makes me readier for facing Him.
- Without a belief in my programme and without an acceptance of my condition, you will ruin me, ruin yourselves and ruin the cause.
- All faiths constitute a revelation of truth, but all are imperfect and liable to error.
- Tolerance implies a gratuitous assumption of the inferiority of other faiths to one's own.
- What faith can you place in a general or a soldier who lacks resolution and determination, who says, "I shall keep guard as long as I can?"
- Can a general fight on the strength of the soldiers who, he knows, have no faith in him?
- Decency requires that when a programme is approved by the majority, all should carry it out faithfully.

- Even as a tree has a single trunk, but many branches and leaves, there is one religion but any number of faiths.
- He who would in his own person test the fact of God's presence can do so by a living faith.
- If you have no character to lose, people will have no faith in you.
- Khaddar is an activity that can absorb all the time of all invisible men and women and grown-up children, if they have faith.
- Legal imposition avoids the necessity of honour or good faith.
- The Khadi spirit means an equally illimitable faith.
- Prayer is impossibility without a living faith in the presence of God within.
- The renunciation of the Gita is the acid test of faith.
- Those who are lacking in bhakti (devotion), lacking in faith, are all disqualified to interpret the scriptures.

Fast (Fasting)

- Fasting and prayer are common injunctions in my religion.
- Fasting for light and penance is a hoary institution.
- A pure fast, like duty, is its own reward.
- Fasting is an institution as old as Adam. It has been resorted to for self-purification or for some ends, noble as well as ignoble.
- A complete fast is a complete and literal denial of selfishness. It is the truest prayer.
- A genuine fast cleanses the body, mind and soul. It crucifies the flesh and to that extent sets the soul free.
- Fasts could not be undertaken out of anger. Anger was a short madness.
- All fasting and all penance must as far as possible be secret.

- What the eyes are for the outer world, fasts are for the inner.
- A fast to be true must be accompanied by a readiness to receive pure thoughts and determination to resist all Satan's temptations.
- When a man fasts, it is not the gallons of water he drinks that sustains him, but God.
- My fast is among other things meant to qualify me for achieving that equal and selfless love.
- My fast is a matter between God and myself.
- My religion teaches me that wherever there is distress, which one cannot remove, one must fast and pray.

Fear (Fearlessness)

- Fear is a worse disease than malaria or kalaazar; these diseases kill the body; fear kills the soul.
- Fear of disease killed more men than disease itself.
- A fear-stricken person can never know God, and one who knows God will never fear a mortal man.
- The fear of the judge within is more terrible than that of the one without.
- Where there is fear, there is no religion.
- There is always the fear of self-righteousness possessing us, the fear of arrogating to ourselves a superiority that we do not possess.
- It is weakness which breeds fear, and fear breeds distrust.
- There would be no one to frighten you if you refused to be afraid.
- The man who fears man falls from the estate of man. Fear God alone.
- The greatest help you can give me is to banish fear from your hearts.
- External fears cease of their own accord when once we have conquered these traitors within the camp.
- For a non-violent person, the whole world is one family. He will thus fear none, nor will others fear him.
- Power is of two kinds. One is obtained by the fear of

punishment and the other by acts of love.

- Power based on love is a thousand times more effective and permanent than the one derived from fear of punishment.
- A man who throws himself on God ceases to fear man.
- Running away for fear of death, leaving one's dear ones, temples or music to take care of them, is not religion; it is cowardice.
- It needs more than a heart of oak to shed all fear except the fear of God.
- You will find that God is always by the side of the fearless. Therefore, we should fear Him alone and seek His protection.
- The golden rule is to act fearlessly upon what one believes to be right.
- Fearlessness presupposes calmness and peace of mind.

Fight

- I am convinced that the masses do not want to fight if the leader does not.
- My fight against untouchability is a fight against the impure in humanity.

Fire

An incendiary uses fire for his destructive ad and nefarious purpose; a housewife makes daily use of it in preparing nourishing food for mankind.

Flag

A national spirit is necessary for the national existence. A flag is a material aid to the development of such a spirit.

Flattery

Flattery and anger are the two sides of weakness, one the obverse, other the reverse, the reverse—anger—is worse than the obverse—flattery.

Force

- Love is the subtlest force in the world.
- The force of non-violence is infinitely more wonderful and subtle than the material forces of Nature, like electricity.
- The force generated by non-violence is infinitely greater than the force of all the arms invented by man's ingenuity.
- The truth is that God is the force. He is the essence of life. He is pure and undefiled consciousness. He is eternal.
- To conquer the subtle passions seems to me to be harder than the physical conquest of the world by the force of arms.
- The older men should yield with grace what will be taken from them by force if they do not read the signs of the times.
- The more efficient a force is the more silent and the more subtle it is.

Foreign cloth

- Love of foreign cloth has brought foreign domination, pauperism and what is worst, shame to many a home.
- Untouchability of foreign cloth is as much a virtue with all of us as untouchability of the suppressed classes must be a sin with every devout Hindu.
- In burning my foreign cloths, I burn my shame.

Forgiveness

- Forgiveness is the quality of the brave, not of the cowardly.
- Forgiveness is a quality of the soul and, therefore, a positive quality.
- The weak can never forgive. Forgiveness is the attribute of the strong.
- A definite forgiveness would mean a definite recognition of one is strength.

- Abstinence is forgiveness only when there is power to punish; it is meaningless when it pretends to proceed from a helpless creature.
- A mouse hardly forgives a cat when it allows itself to be torn to pieces by her.
- Forgiveness adorns a soldier.
- With enlightened forgiveness must come a mighty wave of strength in us, which could make it impossible for a Dyer and a Frank Johnson to heap affront on India's devoted head.

Freedom

- Freedom of a nation cannot be won by solitary acts of heroism though they may be of the true type, never by heroism so-called.
- Freedom is like birth. Till we are fully free, we are slaves.
- Freedom of worship, even of public speech, would become a farce if interference became the order of the day.
- Freedom received through the efforts of others, however benevolent, cannot be retained when such effort is withdrawn.
- Freedom battles are not fought without paying heavy prices.
- No charter of freedom will be worth looking at which does not ensure the same measure of freedom for the minorities as for the majority.
- No government on earth can make men, who have realised freedom in their hearts, salute against their will.
- No society can possibly be built on a denial of individual freedom.
- When freedom is in jeopardy, non-co-operation may be a duty and poison may be a palace.
- God demands nothing less than complete self-surrender as the price for the only real freedom that is worth having.
- Is it not possible for us all to realise that the masses will

never mount to freedom through murder?

- True ahimsa should mean a complete freedom from ill-will and anger and hate and an overflowing love for all.
- The bomb-throwers have discredited the cause of freedom, in whose name they threw the bombs.
- There is nothing but non-violence to fall back upon for retaining our freedom, even as we had to do for gaining it.
- This freedom from all attachment is the realisation of God as truth.
- Freedom of India will demonstrate to all the exploited races of the earth that their freedom is very near.
- India's freedom will not be won by violence but only by the patient suffering without retaliation.
- There is every reason for being cautious about founding new universities till India has digested the newly acquired freedom.
- We want freedom for our country, but not at the expense or exploitation of others, not so as to degrade other countries.
- I do not want my house to be walled in on all sides and my windows to be stuffed. I want the cultures of all the lands to be blown about my house as freely as possible.
- If any Englishman dedicated his life to securing the freedom of India, resisting tyranny and serving the land, I should welcome that Englishman as an Indian.
- I would willingly see India perish rather that she won freedom by the sacrifice of truth.
- I would not sell the vital interests of the untouchables for the sake of winning the freedom of India.
- My interest in India's freedom will cease if she adopts violent means, for their fruit will not be freedom but slavery in disguise.
- For my own part, I do not want the freedom of India if it means extinction of England or the disappearance of Englishmen.

- Through realisation of freedom of India, I hope to realise and carry on the mission of brotherhood of men.
- It will be hard to find a parallel in history in which unarmed people have represented the urge for freedom, turning the very unarmedness into the central means for deliverance.
- Though we are politically free, we are hardly free from the subtle domination of the west.
- Nothing depends upon the death of an individual be he ever so great, but much depends upon the freedom of India.
- A slave has not the freedom even to do the right thing.
- A slave-leader, who has decided to abolish slavery, does not consult his slaves whether they desire freedom or not.

Friends (Friendship)

- Friends to be friends are not called upon to agree even on most points.
- Death is no friend; he is the truest of friends. He delivers us from agony.
- With me marriage is no necessary test of friendship even between husband and wife, let alone their respective clans.
- It is the acid test of non-violence that in a non-violent conflict there is no rancour left behind, and in the end, the enemies are converted into friends.
- My attitude towards the English is one of utter friendliness and respect.

Gandhism

- If Gandhism means simply mechanically turning the spinning wheel it, deserves to be destroyed.
- What is Gandhism but winning Swaraj by means of truth and non-violence?

- There is no such thing as 'Gandhism', and I do not want to leave any sect after me.
- If our ahimsa is not of the brave, and if it will bend the knee before himsa, Gandhism deserves to be destroyed.
- They might kill me, but they cannot kill Gandhism. If truth can be killed, Gandhism can be killed.
- I hold my message to be far superior to myself and far superior to the vehicle through which it is expressed.
- Unless the charkha adds to your ahimsa and makes you stronger every day, your Gandhism is of little avail.
- There is already enough superstition in our country. No effort should be spared to resist further addition in the shape of Gandhi worship.
- Though a non-co-operator, I shall gladly subscribe to a bill to make it criminal for anybody to call me mahatma and to touch my feet.
- Was it that you wanted to pull my leg by transporting me to the frozen Himalayan heights of 'mahatmaship' and claiming for yourself absolution from having to follow my precepts?

General, his weakness

- A general is none the worse for the realisation of his weakness and for atoning for his sin.
- If the commander-in-chief will look beyond the defence forces, he will discover that real India is not military but peace-loving.

Gentleness

Non-violent acts exert pressure far more effective than violent acts, for that pressure comes from goodwill and gentleness.

Germany

- I am not just now thinking of India's deliverance. It will come, but what will be wrought if England and France fall, or if they come out victorious over Germany ruined and humbled.

- I must refuse to believe that the Germans contemplate with equanimity the evacuation of cities like London for fear of destruction to be wrought by man's inhuman ingenuity.

Gifts

- I fear the Greeks especially when they bring gifts.
- What we receive must be called a gift; for as debtors we are entitled to no consideration for the discharge of the obligations.

God

- God accepts the sacrifice of the pure in heart.
- God always saves the world from the consequences of unintended errors of men who live in fear of Him.
- God alone is immortal, imperishable.
- God alone is truth and everything else is transitory and illusory.
- God alone knows absolute truth.
- God answers prayer in His own way, not ours.
- God as truth has been for me a treasure beyond price; may He be so to every one of us.
- God can never be realised by one who is not pure of heart.
- God cannot be as cruel and unjust as to make the distinctions of high and low between man and man, and woman and woman.
- God cannot be realised through the intellect.
- God chooses as His instrument the humblest and weakest of His creatures to fulfill himself.
- God created man to work for his food and said that those who ate without work were thieves.
- God demands nothing less than self-surrender as the price for the only freedom that is worth having.
- God does not punish directly. His ways are inscrutable.

- God gifted man with intellect that he might know his maker. Man abused it so that he might forget his maker.
- God-given religion is beyond all speech.
- God has a thousand names, or rather He is nameless.
- God has been described by all the scriptures of the world a protector and saviour of the sinner.
- God has blessed men with seed that has the highest potency and woman with a field richer than the richest earth to be found anywhere on his globe.
- God has blessed me with the mission to place non-violence before the nation for adoption.
- God has enabled man to distinguish between his sister, his mother, his daughter and his wife.
- God has enabled me to affect the life of the country since 1920 without the necessity of office.
- God has given us only a limited sphere of action and a limited version.
- God has His own way of choosing His instruments.
- God has made of man and woman one complete whole. In the scheme of Nature, both of them are equal.
- God has so ordered this world that no one can keep his goodness or badness exclusively to himself.
- God having cast my lot in the midst of the people of India, I should be untrue to my maker if I failed to serve them.
- God himself has reserved no right of revision of His own laws nor is there any need for Him for any such revision.
- God is the hardest taskmaster I have known on this earth and He tries you through and through.
- God is the source of light and life, and yet He is above and beyond all these. God is conscience.
- God is the vital force or spirit which is all-pervading, all embracing and, therefore, beyond human ken.
- God is the shield of the non-violent.
- God is always the upholder of justice.
- God is certainly one. He has no second. He is

unfathomable, unknowable and unknown to the vast majority of mankind.

- God is continuously in action, without resting for a single moment.
- God is light, not darkness. God is love, not hate. God is truth, not untruth. God alone is great.
- God is not a person. God is an eternal principle.
- God of truth and justice can never create distinctions of high and low among His own children.
- God resides in every human form, indeed in every particle of His creations, in everything that is on this earth.
- God's laws are eternal and unalterable and not separable from God Himself.
- God's word is: He who strives never perishes.
- God was known by many names. And in the last analysis God's names were as many as human beings.
- I believe in absolute oneness of God and, therefore, also of humanity.
- I claim no perfection for myself. But I do claim to be a passionate seeker after truth, which is but another name for God.
- I know that I can never be alone as God is there with me.
- I recognise no God except the God that is to be found in the hearts of the dumb millions.
- I trust men only because I trust God.
- For me, Rama and Rahim are one and the same deity. I acknowledge no other God but the one God of truth and righteousness.
- I will not be a traitor of God to please the whole world.
- It is my unmistakable belief that not a blade of grass moves but by the divine will.
- My religion is based on truth and non-violence. Truth is my God. Non-violence is the means of realising Him.
- My religion says that only he who is prepared to suffer can pray to God.

- My creed is service of God and, therefore, of humanity.
- My fast is a matter between God and myself.
- My firm belief is that he reveals Himself daily to every human being, but we shut our ears to the still small voice.
- My imperfections and failures are as much a blessing from God as my successes and my talents, and I lay them both at His feet.
- The purer I try to become, the nearer I feel to God.
- To me, truth is God and there is no way to find truth except the way of non-violence.
- To me, God is truth and love; God is ethics and morality; God is fearlessness.
- A fear-stricken person can never know God, and one who knows God will never fear a mortal man.
- A mind not set on God is given to wandering and lacks the quality of a temple of worship.
- A personal selfish prayer is bad whether made before an image or an unseen God.
- As soon as we become one with the ocean in the shape of God, there is no more rest for us, nor indeed do we need rest any longer.
- Assumption of superiority in any person over any other is a sin against God and man.
- Before the throne of the Almighty, man will be judged not by his acts, but by his intentions.
- Celibacy is a great help, in as much as it enables one to lead a life of full surrender to God.
- Conversion without a clean heart is a denial of God and religion.
- Cowardice is not a sign of belief in God.
- Do not worry in the least about yourself; leave all worry to God. This appears to be the commandment in all religions.
- Fight if you must on the path of righteousness and God will be with you.

- If we take care of today, God will take care of tomorrow.
- In a strictly scientific sense God is at the bottom of both good and evil.
- In His boundless love, God permits the atheist to live.
- In the unadulterated belief in the oneness of God and a practical application of the truth of the brotherhood of man for those who are nominally within its fold are two distinctive contribution of Islam.
- In the Gita, continuous concentration on God is the king of sacrifices.
- It is better to be charged with cowardice and weakness than to be guilty of denial of our oath and sin against God.
- It needs more than a heart of oak to shed all fear except the fear of God.
- Let us fear God and we shall cease to fear man.
- Living faith in God means acceptance of the brotherhood of mankind.
- Meditation is waiting on God.
- Man alone is made in the image of God.
- Man can only try and perish in the attempt. God is all in all. We are only zeros.
- The man who eats to live who is a friend with the five powers—earth, water, ether, sun, and air—who is a servant of God, the creator of all these, ought not to fall ill.
- The man who fears man falls from the estate of man. Fear God alone.
- When a man fasts, it is not the gallons of water he drinks that sustains him, but God.
- When a man wants to make up with his maker he does not consult a third party.
- A man cannot serve God and Mammon, nor be 'temperate and furious' at the same time.
- A man of faith does not bargain or stipulate with God.

- A man with a grain of faith in God never loses hope, because he ever believes in the ultimate triumph of truth.
- A man who throws himself on God ceases to fear man.
- Satyagraha is search for truth and God is truth.
- Search for truth is search for God. Truth is God. God is because truth is.
- Shraddha means self-confidence and self-confidence means faith in God.
- Surely, conversion is a matter between man and his maker who alone knows His creatures' hearts.
- That which impels man to do the right is God.
- That which makes man the mere playing of fate is God.
- The idol in the temple is not God. But since God resides in every atom, He resides in an idol.
- The Law which governs all life is God.
- There are innumerable definitions of God because His manifestations are innumerable.
- The sky may be overcast today with clouds, but a fervent prayer to God is enough to dispel them.
- The sum of all that lives is God.
- The sum total of karma is God.
- When we fear God, then we shall fear no man, however high-placed he may be.
- Where love is, there God is also.
- Without an unreserved surrender to His grace, complete mastery over thoughts is impossible.
- You are not going to know the meaning of God or prayer unless you reduce yourself to a cipher.
- If gold were as easily available as iron, it would not for all its glitter have the same value that it has today.
- Not all our gold and jewellery could satisfy our hunger and quench our thirst.

Golden Rule

Judge not lest ye be judged is a golden rule.

Good—Goodness

- The good that man does is more often than not better left unsaid.
- Religion taught us to return good for evil.
- A drop torn from the ocean perishes without doing any good.

Goondas

- Goondas flourish only in the midst of timid people.
- It is we who make the goondas; without our sympathy and passive support goondas would have no legs to stand upon.
- Intolerance is a form of goondaism [hooliganism]. It is no less disgraceful than savagery.

Government

- A government builds its prestige upon the apparently voluntary association of the governed.
- Government of the people by the people and for the people cannot be conducted at the bidding of one man, however great he may be.

Grave

We shall dig our own grave if we do not purge ourselves of this curse of untouchability.

Gravitation

The law of love will work just as the law of gravitation will work, whether we accept it or not.

Greatness

- The greatness to be great has to be lowliest by choice.
- True greatness in the world is not found set upon a hill for the vulgar crowd to see.

- God alone is the judge of true greatness because he knows men's hearts.
- God is light, not darkness. God is love, not hate, God is truth, not untruth, God alone is great.

Handicraft

He who runs may see, if he would also think, that the future lies with craftsmanship.

Handsome

Handsome is not he who is handsomely clothed; handsome is he who handsome does.

Hanuman

Rama was not only on the lips of Hanuman. He was enthroned in his heart. He gave Hanuman exhaustless strength.

Happiness

True art must be evidence of happiness, contentment and purity of its authors.

Harijan

- Harijan service is a duty the upper caste Hindus owe to themselves.
- It is absurd for a single individual to talk of taking all Harijans with himself. Are they all bricks that they be moved from one structure to another?
- The principle of ahimsa is hurt by every evil thought, by undue haste, by lying, by hatred, by wishing ill to anybody.

Hate—Hatred

- Hatred is not essential for nationalism. Race hatred will kill the national spirit.
- The hater hates not for the sake of hatred but because he wants to drive away from his country the hated being or beings.

- Hatred can be overcome only be love. Counter-hatred only increases the surface as well as the depth of hatred.

- I would rather drown myself in the waters of the Sabarmati than harbour hate or animosity in my heart.
- Harshness is conquered by gentleness, hatred by love, lethargy by zeal and darkness by light.
- It is heavy downpour of rain, which drenches the soil to fullness, likewise only a profuse shower of love overcomes hatred.
- It is health, which is real wealth, not pieces of silver and gold.
- A diseased person has a prospect of getting well by personal effort. He cannot borrow health from others.

Helplessness

- It is the privilege of arms to protect the weak and helpless.
- Your trouble is not numerical inferiority but the feeling of helplessness that has seized you and the habit of depending on others.
- Even a bloody war is better than utter helplessness and unmanliness.

Himalayas

- The Himalayas are spotlessly snow-white in virtue of the spotless glory of the countless sages who laid down their lives performing penance in their caves.
- If I could persuade myself that I could find Him in a Himalayan cave, I would proceed there immediately.

Hindi

Highly Sankritised Hindi is as avoidable as Persianised Urdu.

Hindu—Hinduism

- Hinduism dies if untouchability lives, and untouchability

has to die if Hinduism is to live.

- Hinduism does not rest on the authority of one book or one prophet, nor does it possess a common creed like the kalma.
- Hinduism had absorbed the best of all the faiths of the world and in that sense Hinduism was not an exclusive religion.
- Hinduism has sinned in giving sanction to untouchability.
- Hinduism is not a codified religion.
- Hinduism is not an exclusive religion. In it there is room for the worship of all the prophets in the world.
- Hinduism loses its right to make a universal appeal if it closes its temples to the Harijans.
- Hinduism with its message of ahimsa is to me the most glorious religion in the world.
- Cow-protection is an article of faith in Hinduism.
- Cow-protection is the gift of Hinduism to the world.
- My life is dedicated to the service of Indians through the religion of non-violence, which I believe to be the root of Hinduism.
- My respectful study of other religions has not abated my reverence for or my faith in the Hindu scriptures.
- The more I study the Hindu scriptures, and the more I discuss them with Brahmins, the more I feel convinced that untouchability is the greatest blot upon Hinduism.
- If Hinduism teaches hatred of Islam or of non-Hindus, it is doomed to destruction.
- The removal of untouchability is a question of the purification of Hinduism.
- Untouchability is a blot on Hinduism. It is a canker eating into its vitals.
- All the four stages in a man's life are devised by the seers in Hinduism for imposing discipline and self-restraint.
- No stone should be left unturned to bring home to the family members that untouchability is a sin and a blot on Hinduism.

- The scriptures of Christians, Mussalmans and Hindus are all replete with the teaching of ahimsa.
- The only way Hinduism can convert the whole world to cow-protection is by giving an object-lesson in cow-protection and all it means.
- Hindu religious literature, indeed all religious literature, is full of illustrations to prove the truth.
- History is a record of perpetual wars, but we are now trying to make new history.

Hitler

Hitler is awake all the twenty-four hours of the day in perfection of his sadhana.

Honesty

- Honesty has never been so much to be the best policy as it is now for those who do not or cannot back their dishonesty with gun powder and poisonous gas.
- The only real reliable guarantee for khadi would be the honesty, truthfulness and sincerity of khadi workers.
- The method of satyagraha requires that the satyagraha should never lose hope, so long as there is the slightest ground left for it.

Hostility

Differences of opinion should never mean hostility.

Human dignity

It is beneath human dignity to lose one's individuality and become a mere cog in the machine.

Human family

Once we recognise the common parent stock from which we are all sprung, we realise the basic unity of the human family, and there is no room left for enmities and unhealthy competition.

Humanity

I am endeavouring to see God through service of humanity for I know that God is neither in heaven nor down below, but in every one.

Human nature

- Dignity of human nature requires that we must face the storms of life.
- Not to believe in the possibility of permanent peace is to disbelieve in the godliness of human nature.

Humility

- True humility means most strenuous and constant endeavour entirely directed to the service of humanity.
- Non-violence is impossible without humility.

Hunger

- Hunger is the argument that is driving India to the spinning wheel.
- Not all our gold and jewellery could satisfy our hunger and quench our thirst.

Hunger Strike

A hunger strike loses its force and dignity, when it has any, if the striker is forcibly fed.

Hypocrisy

- Hypocrisy and distortion are passing currents under the name of religion.
- Corruption and hypocrisy ought not to be inevitable products of democracy, as they undoubtedly are today.
- Hypocrisy has acted as an ode to virtue but it could never take its place.

Ideal

- The virtue of an ideal consists in its boundlessness.

- Man falls from the pursuit of the ideal of plain living and high thinking the moment he wants to multiply his daily wants.

Idleness

Idleness is the great plague of India.

Illiteracy

Mass illiteracy is India's sin and shame and must be liquidated.

Ignorance

- Age-hardened ignorance cannot yield to a few months' object-lessons.
- My greatest worry is the ignorance and poverty of the masses of India and the way in which they have been neglected by the classes, especially the neglect of the Harijans by the Hindus.

Imitation

No country can become a nation by producing a race of imitators.

Immoral

It is wrong and immoral for a nation to supply intoxicating liquor to those who are addicted to drink.

Immortal

- Science has not so far discovered any recipe for making the body immortal.
- If we must be impatient, we must be impatient with ourselves, not with the wrongdoer.

Imperialists—Imperialism

- The greatest menace to the world today is the growing exploiting irresponsible imperialism.

• Imperialism is a negation of God. It does ungodly acts in the name of God.
• The untouchability of Hinduism is probably worse than that of the modern imperialists.

Imposition

Legal imposition avoids the necessity of honour or good faith.

Impossible

We are daily witnessing the phenomenon of the impossible of yesterday becoming possible of today.

Independence

- I want for India complete independence in the full English sense of that English term.
- Independence means voluntary restraints and discipline voluntary acceptance of the rule of law.
- Complete independence does not mean arrogant isolation or a superior claim for all help.
- We cannot have real independence unless the people banish the touch-me-not spirit from the hearts.
- If it is man's privilege to be independent, it is equally his duty to be inter-dependent.
- Only an arrogant man will claim to be independent, it is equally his duty to be interdependent.

India—Indians

- India must learn to live before she can aspire to die for humanity.
- India is essentially a karmabhumi [land of duty] in contradiction to bhogabhumi [land of enjoyment].
- India has an unbroken tradition of non-violence from time immemorial.
- An India prostrate at the feet of Europe can give no hope to humanity.
- An India free from exploitation from within and without

must prosper with astonishing rapidity.

- If India becomes the slave of the machine, then, I say, heaven save the world.
- India's freedom will not be won by violence but only by the purest suffering without retaliation.
- India's acceptance of the doctrine of the sword will be the hour of my trial.
- India's way is not Europe's. India is not Calcutta and Bombay. India lives in her seven hundred thousand villages.
- Whatever else India may not be, she is at least one thing; she is the greatest storehouse of spiritual knowledge.
- Let India become alive by self-purification, that is self-restraint and self-denial, and she will be a boon to herself and mankind.
- In a self-respecting India, is not every woman's virtue as much every man's concern as his own sister's?
- In the true democracy of India, the unit is the village.
- I do not want India to rise on the ruin of other nations.
- I would far rather that India perished than that she won freedom at the sacrifice of truth.
- I would like to bury myself in an Indian village, preferably in a frontier village.
- Through realisation of freedom of India, I hope to realise and carry on the mission of brotherhood of man.
- I am wedded to India because I owe my all to her.
- I believe in the capacity of India to offer non-violent battle to the English rulers.
- It is my unshakable belief that India's destiny is to deliver the message of non-violence to mankind.
- My interest in India's freedom will cease if she adopts violent means, for their fruit will not be freedom but slavery in disguise.
- In my dream, in my sleep, while eating, I think of the spinning wheel, the spinning wheel is my sword. To me,

it is the symbol of India's liberty.

- I have called spinning the yagya of this age of India.
- A free India will throw all her weight in favour of world disarmament and should herself be prepared to give a lead in this.
- The freedom of India is a bigger thing than the disease, which for the time being is corroding some sections of Indian community.
- With the loss of India to non-violence, the last hope of the world will be gone.
- Drink is not a fashion in India, as it is in the west.
- The British power is the overlord without whom Indian prince cannot breathe.
- Half-a-dozen or twenty cities of India alone working together cannot bring Swaraj.
- The spinning wheel is as much a necessity of Indian life as air and water.
- Khadi to me is the symbol of unity of Indian humanity, of its economic freedom and equality and therefore, ultimately, in the poetic expression of Jawaharlal Nehru, 'the livery of India's freedom.'
- Hunger is the argument that is driving India to the spinning wheel.
- There is no better way of industrialising the villages of India than the spinning wheel.
- Nothing depends upon the death of an individual, be he ever so great, but much depends upon the freedom of India.
- Unity among the different races and the different religions of India is indispensable to the birth of national life.
- Let us remember that we are all Indians eating Indian grain and salt, and living on the dumb Indian masses.
- Mass illiteracy is India's sin and shame and must be liquidated.
- Basic education links the children, whether of the cities

or villages, to all that is best and lasting in India.

- Of all the superstitions that affect India, none is as great as that knowledge of the English language is necessary for imbibing ideas of liberty and developing accuracy of thought.
- If there was any teacher in the world who insisted upon the inexorable law of cause and effect, it was Gautam. The Buddhists outside India would, if they could, avoid the effects of their own acts.
- We Indians are one and not two as Englishmen are.
- The way to Indian independence does not go through the sword but through mutual friendship and adjustment.

Indiscipline

Indiscipline will surely mean disaster, and make one like me, who is pining to see Swaraj in his lifetime, perish in sorrow and grief.

Inequality

- The word 'inequality' has a bad odour about it, and it has led to arrogance and inhumanities both in the East and West.
- Diversity there certainly is in the world, but it means neither inequality nor untouchability.

Injustice

- To call women the weaker sex is a libel; it is man's injustice to women.
- Agitation against every form of injustice is the breath of political life.

Inner Voice

Penances with me are no mechanical acts; they are done in obedience to the inner voice.

Innocent

- The willing sacrifice of the innocent is the most powerful retort to insolent tyranny that has yet been conceived by God or man.
- For infallible guidance man has to have a perfectly innocent heart incapable of evil.

Internationalism

Internationalism is possible only when nationalism becomes a fact.

Intolerance

- All criticism is not intolerance. I have criticised the revolutionary because I have felt for him. He has the same right to hold me to be in error as I believe him to be in error.
- Intolerance of criticism even of what one may prize as dear as life itself is not conducive to the growth of public corporate life.

Islam

- Islam stands for the unity and brotherhood of mankind, and not for disrupting the oneness of the human family.
- Islam was born in an environment where the sword was and still remains the supreme law.
- The very word Islam means peace, which is non-violence.
- A perfect Muslim is he from whose tongue and hands mankind is safe.

Japan

- The atom bomb brought an empty victory to the Allied arms, but it resulted for the time being in destroying the soul of Japan.
- I am convinced that the capitalist, if he follows the Samurai of Japan, has nothing really to lose and everything to gain.

- Let no one run away with the idea that I wish to put in a defence of Japanese misdeeds in pursuance of Japan's unworthy ambition.

Jealousy

- Jealousy presupposes the possibility of rivalry.
- Bury the jealousies underground and cremate them wherever you like.

Journalism

- Journalism has become the art of intelligent anticipation of event.
- The sole aim of journalism should be service.
- Journalism should never be prostituted for selfish ends or for the sake of merely earning livelihood or, worse still, for amassing money.
- Journalism has a distinct place in familiarising and expressing public opinion.
- A journalist's peculiar function is to read the mind of the country and to give definite and fearless expression to that mind.
- The newspaperman has become a walking plague. He spreads the contagion of lies and calumnies.
- The press was called the fourth Estate. It was definitely a power, but to misuse that power was criminal.
- The newspapers should be read for the study of facts. They should not be allowed to kill the habit of independent thinking.
- In the East, as in the West, the newspapers are fast becoming the people's Bible, the Koran, the Zend Avesta and the Gita rolled into one.
- Freedom of the press is a precious privilege that no country can forego.
- An itch for new is a variety of dissipation, debilitating to the mind and spirit, unless it is properly curbed.
- The liberty of the press is a dear privilege, apart from

the advisability or otherwise of civil disobedience.

• The newspapers had become more important to the average man than the scriptures.

Joy

A life of sacrifice is the pinnacle of art, and is full of true joy.

Justice

- Justice should become cheap and expeditious. Today it is the luxury of the rich and the joy of the gambler.
- Justice will come when it is deserved by our being and strong feeling.
- Justice does not help the ones who slumber but helps only those who are vigilant.
- The first condition of non-violence is justice all round, in every department of life.
- It is open to a war-resister to judge between two combatants and wish success to the one who has justice on his side.

Karma Yoga

- This dharma in the original [Gita] refers to Karma Yoga, and the Karma Yoga of our age is the spinning wheel.
- The biggest of Karmayogis never give up devotional songs or worship.

Khadi-Khaddar

- Khadi is the sun of the village solar system.
- Khaddar was conceived with a much more ambitious object, that is, to make our villages starvation-proof.
- The Khadi spirit means fellow feeling with every human being on earth.
- The khadi spirit means also an infinite patience.
- Khaddar does not displace a single cottage industry.
- Khaddar delivers the poor from the bonds of the rich

and creates a moral and spiritual bond between the classes and the masses.

- Khaddar brings a ray of hope to the widow's broken up home.
- Khaddar has the greatest organising power in it, because it has itself to be organised and because it affects all India.
- Khaddar is an activity that can absorb all the time of all available men and women and grown-up children if they have faith.
- Khadi service, village service and the Harijan service are one in reality, though three in name.
- Khadi mentality means decentralisation of the production and distribution of the necessities of life.
- Khadi has been conceived as the foundation and the image of ahimsa. A real khadi-wearer will not utter an untruth. A real khadi-wearer will harbour no violence, no deceit and no impurity.
- I had bargained for a khaddar hut, but I was insulted with a khaddar palace.
- I would ask upon to come in khadi, for khadi links you with the fallen and the downtrodden.
- Even if masses of people were to burn khadi publicly and say that it is an insane programme, I will declare that those people have gone mad.
- My Swadeshi chiefly centres round the hand-spun khaddar and extend to everything that can be and is produced in India.
- Khaddar of my conception is that hand-spun fabric, which takes entirely the place of mill cloth in India.
- Khadi will cease to have any value in my eyes if it does not usefully employ the millions.
- All the other industries will receive warmth and sustenance from khadi industry.
- Boycott brought about anyhow of British cloth cannot yield the same results as such boycott brought about by hand spinning and khaddar.

- Coal is not dear for the coal-miner who can use it there and then, nor is khadi dear for the villager who maunfactures his own khadi.
- Even as Satyagraha is a weapon unique of the kind and not one of the ordinary weapons used by people, so is khadi a unique article of commerce, which will not, cannot, succeed on terms common to other articles.
- For a firm believer in swadeshi, there need be no pharisaical self-satisfaction in wearing khadi.
- If we have the khadi spirit in us, then we should surround ourselves with simplicity in every walk of life.
- Organisation of Khaddar is infinitely better than co-operative societies of any other form of village organisation.
- The art that is in the machine-made article, appeals only to the eye; the art in Khadi appeals first to the heart and then to the eye.
- The foundation of service and your real training lies in spinning khaddar.
- The khadi work without the mastery of the science of khadi will be love's labour lost in terms of Swaraj.
- The message of khaddar can penetrate to the remotest villages if we only will that it shall be so.
- The only real and reliable guarantee for khadi would be the honesty, truthfulness and sincerity of khadi workers.
- The singular secret of khaddar lies in its saleability in the place of its production and use by the manufactures themselves.
- Through khadi, we teach the people the art of civil obedience to an institution, which they have built up for themselves.
- Without proper careful organisation of the spinning wheel and khaddar, there is absolutely no civil disobedience.

Kisan

- No one tells the cultivator to take breathing exercise or to work his muscles.
- The Congress is nothing if it does not represent the *kisan*.

Knowledge

- Knowledge without devotion will be like a misfire.
- Knowledge and devotion, to be true, have to stand the test of renunciation of the fruits of action.
- True knowledge gives a moral standing and moral strength.
- Krishna of the Gita is perfection and right knowledge personified; but the picture is imaginary.
- What will tell in the end will be character and not a knowledge of letters.
- Without devotion, action and knowledge are cold and dry and many even become shackles.
- Knowledge of the tallest scientist or the greatest spiritualist is like a particle of dust.
- One rupee can purchase for us poison or nectar, but knowledge or devotion cannot buy us either salvation or bondage.
- In order that knowledge may not run riot, the author of the Gita has insisted on devotion accompanying it and has given it the first place.
- The renunciation is the central sun, round which devotion knowledge and the rest revolve like planets.
- My varnashrama refuses to bow the head before the greatest potentate on earth, but my varnashrama compels me to bow down my head in all humility before knowledge, purity before every person where I see God face to face.

Labour

- Capital exploits the labour of a few to multiply itself.

- Every labourer is worthy of his hire. No country can produce thousands of unpaid whole time workers.
- Is not labour, like learning, its own reward?
- Labour has its unique place in a cultured human family.
- Labour was priceless, not gold.
- Labour was a great leveller of all distinctions.
- No labour is too mean for one who wants to earn an honest penny.
- There is a world-wide conflict between capital and labour, and the poor envy the rich.
- The saving of labour of the individual should be the object and honest humanitarian considerations, and not greed, the motive.
- Unless our heads go hand-in-hand with our hands, we would be able to do nothing whatsoever.
- Useful manual labour, intelligently performed, is the means par excellence for developing the intellect.
- I do not regard capital to be the enemy of labour.
- I call myself a labourer because I take pride in calling myself a spinner, weaver, farmer and scavenger.
- A labourer cannot sit at the table and write, but a man who has worked at the table all his life can certainly take to physical labour.
- A plea of the spinning wheel is a plea for recognising the dignity of labour.
- A scavenger who works in His service shares equal distinction with a king who uses his gift in His name and as a mere trustee.
- A true and non-violent combination of labour would act like a magnet attracting to it all the needed capital.
- A worker's capital is inexhaustible, incapable of being stolen, and bound to pay him a generous dividend all the time.
- Each and every one of you should consider himself to be a trustee for the welfare of the rest of his fellow

labourers and not be self-seeking.

- If everybody lives by the sweat of his brow, the earth will become a paradise.
- It is a sad thing that our school boys look upon manual labour with disfavour, if not contempt.
- Labour, because it chose to remain unintelligent, either became subservient, or insolently believed in damaging the capitalists' goods and machinery or even in killing the capitalists.
- Mere mental, that is, intellectual labour is for the soul and is its own satisfaction.
- Nothing will demoralise the nation so much as that we should learn to despise labour.
- Our children should not be so taught as to despise labour.
- Obedience to the law of bread labour will bring about a silent revolution in the structure of society.
- The employers ganging up against the workers are like raising an army of elephants against ants.
- The rich cannot accumulate wealth without the co-operation of the poor in society.
- This mad rush for wealth must cease and the labourer must be assured not only of living wage, but a daily task that is not a mere drudgery.
- What the two hands of the labourer could achieve, the capitalist would never get with all his gold and silver.
- Where there are millions upon millions of units of idle labour, it is no use to think of the labour-saving devices.

Language

- A language is an exact reflection of the character and growth of its speakers.
- Language is at best an imperfect medium of expression. No man can fully express in words what he feels or thinks.
- The language of a people who produce hard workers,

literary experts, businessmen and enterprising persons spreads and is enriched.

- It is rarely that language succeeds as a vehicle of thought. More often than not, it conceals thought. Always language circumscribes thought.
- There never was a greater superstition than that a particular language can be incapable of expansion or expressing abstruse scientific ideas.
- Man can only describe God in his own poor language.
- If we have listening ears, God speaks to us in our own language, whatever that language be.
- When we start receiving education through our own language, our relations in the home will take on a different character.

Law

- The law which governs all life is God.
- The law is God. Anything attributed to Him is not a mere attribute. He is Truth, Love, Law and a million things that human ingenuity can name.
- The law and the lawgiver are one.
- Affection cannot be manufactured or regulated by law.
- The laws of nature are changeless, unchangeable, and there are no miracles in the sense of infringement or interruption of nature's law.
- A Satyagrahi cannot go to law for a personal wrong.
- Where death without resistance or death after resistance is the only way, neither party should think of resorting to law courts or help from Government.
- The recognition of the golden rule of never taking the law into one's own hands has no exceptions.
- Independence meant voluntary restraint and discipline, voluntary acceptance of the rule of law.
- When there is war the poet lays down the lyre, the lawyer his law reports the school boy his books.

Leaders

An institution that suffers from a plethora of leaders is surely in a bad way.

Learning

- Learning takes us through many stages in life, but it fails us utterly in the hours of danger and temptation.
- Persistent questioning and healthy inquisitiveness are the first requisite for acquiring learning of any kind.
- In a democratic scheme, money invested in the promotion of learning gives a ten-fold return to the people, even as a seed sown in good soil returns a luxuriant crop.

Legislatures

Truth and non-violence are both the means, and the end, and given the right type of men, the legislatures can be the means of achieving the concrete pursuit of truth and non-violence.

Liberation

All the India scriptures have certainly preached incessantly liberation as an immediate aim, but we know that activity in the lower worlds is being abandoned.

Liberty

- Liberty is a dearly bought commodity and prisons are factories where it is manufactured.
- Liberty never meant the licence to do anything at will.
- A rose will smell as sweet by any other name, but it must be the rose of liberty that I want and not the artificial product.
- We dare not enter the kingdom of liberty with mere lip homage to truth and non-violence.
- No power on earth could resist the lovers of liberty who were ready not to kill opponents, but be killed by them.

- Individual liberty is allowed to man only to a certain extent. He cannot forget that he is a social being and his individual liberty has to be curtailed at every step.
- Individual liberty and interdependence are both essential for life in society.
- The one condition for fighting for peace and liberty is to acquire self-restraint.

Life

- A life without vows is like a ship without an anchor or like an edifice that is built on sand instead of a solid rock.
- Life is greater than all art.
- Life becomes livable only to the extent that death is treated as a friend, never as an enemy.
- Life is an aspiration. Its mission is to strive after perfection, which is self-realisation.
- A life of sacrifice is the pinnacle of art, and is full of true joy.
- Human life is a service of compromises, and it is not always easy to achieve in practice what one has found to be true in theory.
- Our life is a long and arduous quest after truth, and the soul requires inward restfulness to attain its full height.
- The music of life is in danger of being lost in the music of the voice.
- A true life lived amongst the people is in itself an object lesson that must produce its own effect upon immediate surroundings.
- What is life worth without trials and tribulations, which are the salt of life.
- The Enlightened one has told you in never-to-be-forgotten words that this little span of life is but a passing shadow, a fleeting thing.
- I believe in God, not as a theory but as a fact more real than that of life itself.
- I want to realise brotherhood or identify not merely with

the being called human, but I want to realise identity with all life, even with such beings as crawl on earth.

- My dharma teaches me to give my life for the sake of others without even attempting to kill.
- My faith in truth and non-violence is ever growing, and as I am ever trying to follow them in my life, I too am growing every moment.
- Let the Gita be to you a mine of diamonds, as it has been to me, let it be your constant guide and friends on life's way.
- Domestic matters are trifles for me. But they occupy the principal part of my life. They teach me to know my limitation.
- The only praise I would like and treasure is the promotion of the activities to which my life is dedicated.
- Healthy well-informed, balanced criticism is the ozone of public life.
- Every single act of one who would lead a life of purity should be in the nature of yagya.
- The secret of happy life lies in renunciation. Renunciation is life.
- Man is sent into the world to perform his duty even at the cost of his life.
- To know music is to transfer it to life.
- Let us give today first the vital things of life and all grace and ornaments of life will follow.
- Dignity of human nature requires that we must face the storms of life.
- Individual liberty and interdependence are both essential for life in society.

Literacy

- Literacy in itself is no education.
- Literacy is not the end of education, or even the beginning.

Love

- Love and ahimsa are matchless in their effect.
- Love in the sense of ahimsa had only a limited number of votaries in the world.
- Love is a rare herb that makes a friend even of a sworn enemy and this herb grows out of non-violence.
- Love is no love, which asks for a return.
- The law of love knows no bounds of space or time.
- Love is the subtlest force in the world.
- Love is needed to strengthen the weak; love becomes tyrannical when it exacts obedience from an unbeliever.
- Where love is, there also is God.
- Where there is love, there is life; hatred leads to destruction.
- Mutual trust and mutual love are no trust and no love.
- My love of nationalism is that my country may become free, that if need be the whole of the country die, so that the human race may live.
- God is light, not darkness, God is love, not hate. God is truth, not untruth. God alone is Great.
- Power based on love is a thousand time more effective and permanent than the one derived from fear of punishment.
- Power is of two kinds—one is obtained by the fear of punishment and the other by acts of love.
- A seeker after truth, a follower of the law of love, cannot hold anything against tomorrow.
- The call of the spinning wheel is the noblest of all, because it is the call of love and love is Swaraj.

Machine—Machinery

- The spinning wheel is itself an exquisite piece of machinery. My head bows daily in reverence to its unknown inventor.
- The machine should not be allowed to cripple the limbs of man.

- I would not weep over the disappearance of machinery or consider it a calamity.

Mahabharata

- The author of the Mahabharata has not established the necessity of physical warfare; on the contrary he has proved its futility.
- I regard Duryodhana and his party as the base impulses in man and Arjuna and his party as the higher impulses.

Mahatma

I have never, even in my dream, thought that I was Mahatma and that others were alpatma.

Man—Mankind

- A man who throws himself on God ceases to fear man.
- Man believes and lives.
- Man can only describe God in his own poor language.
- Man is sent into the world to perform his duty even at the cost of his life.
- The more a man gives his life, the more he saves it.
- Man's triumph will consist in substituting the struggle for existence by a struggle for mutual service.
- Man does not live by destruction.
- Man cannot breathe with borrowed lungs.
- Man does not live by bread alone. Many prefer self-respect to food.
- Men of stainless character and self-purification will easily inspire confidence and automatically purify the atmosphere around them.
- Man becomes not the lord and master of all creation, but he is its servant.
- Man is the maker of his own destiny, and I, therefore, ask you to become makers of your own destinies.
- A courageous man prefers death to the surrender of self-respect.
- Bravery is not man's monopoly.

- Man is born of woman; he is flesh of her flesh and bone of her bone.
- Man cannot be transformed from bad to good overnight.
- It is my firm faith that man is by nature going higher.
- I believe in conversion of mankind, not its destruction.
- I hold no man to be indispensable for the welfare of the country.
- I trust man only because I trust God.
- God's ways are more than man's arithmetic.
- God is certainly one. He has no second. He is unfathomable, unknowable and unknown to the vast majority of mankind.
- Every man has an equal right to the necessities of life even as birds and beasts have.
- A selfish basis would not serve the purpose of taking a man higher along the paths of evolution.
- All the great religions of the world inculcate the equality and brotherhood of mankind and the virtue of tolerance.
- Living faith in God means acceptance of the brotherhood of mankind.
- Human language can but imperfectly describe God's ways.
- A man without religion is like a ship without a rudder.
- That which is inherent in man is his virtue.
- Men are good. But they are poor victims making themselves miserable under the false belief that they are doing good.
- Truth is superior to man's wisdom.
- Imperfect men have no right to judge other imperfect men.
- Cow-slaughter and man-slaughter are in my opinion the two sides of the same coin.
- To hear all kinds of tortures without a murmur of resentment is not possible for a human being without the strength that comes from God.

- What is impossible with man is child's play with God.
- Unlike the animal, God has given man the faculty of reason.
- Speed is not the end of life. Man sees more and lives more truly by walking to his duty.

- Marriage is a matter of choice.
- Undefiled love between husband and wife takes one nearer God than any other love.
- Those marriages which are undertaken for the sake of joint service carry their own blessings.

Masses

- Nothing can so quickly put the masses on their legs as the spinning wheel and all it means.
- Character alone will have real effect on the masses.

Millions

- The hungry millions ask for the invigorating food.
- It is a tragedy of the first magnitude that the millions have ceased to use their hands as hands.

Mind

Man can only conceive God within the limitations of his own mind.

Minority

- In a well-ordered society, there should be no minority.
- My non-violence bids me dedicate myself to the service of the minorities.

Misdeeds

Let us learn from the English rulers the simple fact that the oppressors are blind to the enormity of their own misdeeds.

Mistrust

Trusting one another, however, can mean trusting with the lip and mistrusting in the heart.

Mobocracy

- Mobocracy is autocracy multiplied million times.
- Nothing is so easy as to train mobs, for the simple reason that they have no mind, no meditation.

Moral Force—Morality

- To observe morality is to attain mastery over our mind and our passions.
- To me God is truth and love, God is ethics and morality, God is fearlessness.
- The popular government wields a moral force, which is infinitely superior to the physical force that the foreign government could summon to its assistance.

Mortification

Mortification of the flesh has been held all the world over as a condition of spiritual progress.

Mother—Motherhood

- My mother was certainly a scavenger inasmuch as she cleaned me when I was a child.
- Only a prospective mother knows what it is to carry. The onlookers notice her illness and pity her. But she alone knows the travail.

Mother Tongue

I must cling to my mother-tongue as is my mother's breast, in spite of its shortcomings. It alone can give me the life-giving milk.

Murder

Is it not possible for us all to realise that masses will never mount to freedom through murder?

Museums

Museums of ancient things, which have disappeared from our economic life, have their use and place, but not in our programme, which concentrates on industries and crafts that are capable of being revived.

Music

- The music of life is in danger of being lost in the music of the voice.
- The art of producing good music from a cultivated voice can be achieved by many, but the art of producing that music from the harmony of a pure life is achieved very rarely.
- To know music is to transfer it to life.

Nation (National, Nationalism)

- No nation being under another nation can accept gifts and kick at the responsibility attaching to these gifts, imposed by the conquering nation.
- That nation is great, which rests its head upon death as its pillow.
- Nations are not formed in a day; the formation requires years.
- No country can become a nation by producing a race of imitators.
- My national service is part of my training for freeing my soul from the bondage of flesh.
- The spinning wheel means national consciousness and a contribution by every individual of a definite constructive national work.
- Nationalism, like virtue, was its own reward.

Nature

- Nature abhors weakness.
- Nature has everything for everyone's need, not for everyone's greed.

Nature Cure

- In nature cure, everybody can be his or her own doctor, not so the various systems of medicine.
- Nature care implies that the treatment should be the cheapest and the simplest possible.
- The man who accepts Nature cure never begs.

Non-cooperation

- Non-cooperation is the quickest method of creating public opinion.
- Non-cooperation is protest against an unwritten and unwilling participation in evil.
- Non-cooperation is an attempt to awaken the masses to a sense of their dignity and power.
- Non-cooperation is the nation's determination to improve.
- Non-cooperation means nothing less than training in self-sacrifice.
- Non-co-operation in itself is unnatural, vicious and sinful.
- The Bhagavadgita is a gospel of non-cooperation between the forces of darkness and those of light.
- The nation's non-cooperation is an invitation to the Government to cooperate with it on its own terms, as is every nation's right and every good government's duty.
- Non-cooperation is not a hymn of hate.
- In the very act of my non-cooperation, I am seeking their co-operation in my campaign.
- We must treat arrest as the normal condition of the life of a non-cooperator.
- Non-violence is the rock on which the whole structure of non-cooperation is built.

* For Satyagraha and its offshoots, non-co-operation and civil resistance, are nothing but new names for the law of suffering.

Non-violence

* Non-violence is universal law acting under all circumstances.
* Non-violence is impossible without humility.
* Non-violence is a quality not of the body but of the soul.
* Truth and non-violence are as old as the hills.
* Non-violence abhors fear and, therefore, secrecy.
* True non-violence is mightier than the mightiest violence.
* Non-violence is the summit of bravery.
* Non-violence of the strong is infinitely braver than their violence.
* Non-violence requires great patience.
* Non-violence is the greatest force at the disposal of mankind.
* The charkha is an outward symbol of truth and non-violence.
* God has blessed me with the mission to place non-violence before the nation for adoption.
* Non-violence becomes meaningless if violence is permitted for self-defence.
* You can return blow for blow if you are not brave enough to follow the path of non-violence.
* Non-violence to be a creed has to be all pervasive.
* Non-violence is the virtue of the manly. The cowards are ignorant of it.
* Non-violence is the means; the end for everyone is complete independence.
* A person who believes in non-violence believes in a living God. He cannot accept defeat.
* It is much more difficult to live for non-violence than to die for it.

- Non-violence, which is a quality of the heart, cannot come by an appeal to the brain.
- Non-violence is an attribute of the soul and, therefore, to be practised by everybody in all the affairs of life.
- Non-violence is a universal principle and its operation is not limited by a hostile environment.
- Non-violence is an unchangeable creed. It has to be pursued even in face of violence raging around you.
- The bravery of the non-violent is vastly superior to that of the violent.
- We can't build non-violence in a factory civilisation but it can be built in self-contained villages.
- The patriotic spirit demands loyal and strict adherence to non-violence and truth.
- Love is a rare herb that makes a friend even of a sworn enemy and their herb glows out of non-violence.
- The first step in non-violence is that we cultivate in our daily life, as between ourselves, truthfulness, humility, tolerance and loving kindness.
- The sages, who discovered the law of non-violence in the midst of violence, were greater geniuses than Newton.
- Non-violence is an unchangeable creed.
- Appreciation of non-violence means patient research and still more patient and difficult practice.
- Non-violence in its dynamic condition means conscious suffering.
- The practice of truth and non-violence melted the religious differences, and we learnt to see beauty in each religion.
- The spirit of the Gita teaches the secret of non-violence, the secret of realising self-through the physical body.
- When non-violence is accepted as the law of life, it must pervade the whole being and not be applied to isolated acts.
- A rabbit that runs away from the bull-terrier is not

particularly non-violent.

- Tolstoy was the greater apostle of non-violence that the present age has produced.
- All society is held together by non-violence even as the earth is held in her position by gravitation.
- To practise non-violence in mundane matters is to know its true value.
- Non-violence cannot be learnt by staying at home.
- Non-violence is the first article of my faith. It is also the last article of my creed.
- My religion is based on truth and non-violence. Truth is my God. Non-violence is the means of realising Him.
- My creed of non-violence does not favour the punishment of thieves and dacoits and even murderers.
- My life is dedicated to the service of India through the religion of non-violence, which I believe to be the root of Hinduism.
- My dharma teaches me for the sake of others to give my life without even attempting to kill.
- To my mind, Swaraj based on non-violence is the fulfillment of the constructive programme.
- To me, truth is God and there is no way to find truth except the way of non-violence.
- Truth is my God. I can only search them through non-violence and in no other way.
- The spinning wheel is the symbol of non-violence for me.
- My creed of non-violence is an extremely active force.
- It is my unshakable belief that India's destiny is to deliver the message of non-violence to mankind.
- The only virtue I want to claim is truth and non-violence.
- I have no weapon but non-violence.
- I shall, of course, die with non-violence on my lips.
- I believe in the capacity of India to offer non-violent battle to the English rulers.

- I am a seasoned soldier of non-violence, and I have evidence enough to sustain my faith.
- The non-violent man automatically becomes a servant of God.
- Non-violent action means mobilisation of the world opinion in our favour.
- Non-violence is the rock on which the whole structure of non-cooperation is built.
- For a non-violent person, the whole world is one family. He will thus fear none, nor will others fear him.
- If all were non-violent, there could be no anarchy and there would be no question of anybody arming for meeting aggression from without.
- Those who are truthful, non-violent and brave do not cease to be so because of the stupidity of their leader.

Obedience

- Obedience to the law of bread labour will bring about a silent revolution in the structure of society.
- Compulsory obedience to master is a state of slavery; willing obedience to one's father is the glory of sonship.
- Before civil disobedience can be practised on a vast scale, people must learn of the civil or voluntary obedience.
- Reasoned and willing obedience to the laws of the state is the first lesson in non-cooperation.
- A wretched parent, who claims obedience from his children without first doing his duty to them, excites nothing but contempt.
- Democracy comes naturally to him who is habituated normally to yield willing obedience to all laws, human or divine.
- In a non-violent army, the general and the officers are elected, or are as if elected when their authority is moral and rests solely on the willing obedience of the rank and file.
- Through Khadi we teach the people the art of civil obedience to an institution, which they have built up for themselves.

Ocean

- The ocean is composed of drops of water; each drop is an entity and yet it is part of the whole 'the one and the many'.
- Absolute calm is not the law of ocean. And it is the same with the ocean of life.

Oppression

Everyone should realise the secret that oppression thrived only when the oppressed submitted to it.

Optimist

I am an irrepressible optimist, but I always base my optimism on solid facts.

Organisation

- Organisation like men, if they are to command respect and grow, must have a sense of honour and must fulfill their promises.
- Personal likes and dislikes, ambitions and petty jealousies should have no place in Congress organisation.

Orthodox

The only way by which you and I can wean orthodox Hindus from their bigotry is by patient argument and correct conduct.

Parliament

Parliamentary work is but a minor item of the Congress Programme.

Passion

- By reckless indulgence in their passions, parents serve for their children as models for unrestrained licence.
- To conquer the subtle passions seems to me to be far harder than the physical conquest of the world by the force of arms.

Passive Resistance

- Passive resistance is a method of securing rights by personal suffering; it is the reverse of resistance by arms.
- Passive resistance is an attitudinal all-sided sword; it can be used anyhow; it blesses him who uses it and him against whom it is used.
- Passive resistance, unlike non-violence, has no power to change men's hearts.
- To lose patience is to lose the battle.

Patient

A doctor who uses his talent to pander to the vices of his patient degrades himself and his patient.

Patriotism

- My patriotism is not an exclusive thing. It is all embracing and I should reject that patriotism, which sought to mount upon the distress or exploitation of other nationalities.
- By patriotism I mean the welfare of the whole people, and if I could secure it at the hands of the English, I should bow down my head to them.

Peace

- Without prayer there is no inward peace.
- Prayer is the only means of bringing about orderliness and peace and repose in our daily acts.
- Salvation of the Gita is perfect peace.
- The one condition for fighting for peace and liberty is to acquire self-restraint.

People

- A true life lived amongst the people is in itself an object lesson that must produce its own effect upon immediate surroundings.

- A nation's culture resides in the hearts and in the soul of its people.

Perfect (Perfection)

- Men will ever remain imperfect and it will always be his part to try to be perfect.
- Krishna of the Gita is perfection and right knowledge personified, but the picture is imaginary.
- Life is an aspiration. Its mission is to strive after perfection, which is self-realisation.

Pledge

A religious person will never feel happy in forcing a person to break his pledge of associating himself with such an effort.

Politics (Political)

- Politics divorced from religion has absolutely no meaning.
- Remember that no political programme can stand without the constructive programme.
- Non-violence in politics is a new weapon in the process of evolution. Its vast possibilities are yet unexplored.
- I would dance with joy if I had to give up politics.
- I have sacrificed no principle to gain a political advantage.

Pomp

Pomp and pageantry are often synonymous with vulgarity.

Poor (Poverty)

- Let there be no distinction between rich and poor, high and low.
- The spinning wheel and the spinning wheel alone will solve, if anything will solve, the problem of the deepening poverty of India.

Possible

We are daily witnessing the phenomenon of the impossible of yesterday becoming the possible of today.

Power

- Power is of two kinds. One is obtained by the fear of punishment and the other by acts of love.
- There is an indefinable mysterious power that pervades everything.
- God is not a power residing in the clouds. God is an unseen power residing within us and nearer to us than fingernails to the flesh.
- Man has always desired power. Ownership of property gives this power. Man hankers also after posthumous fame based on power.
- No power on earth can subjugate you when you are armed with the sword of ahimsa.

Prayer

- Prayer is a confession of one's unworthiness and weakness.
- Prayer is the key of the morning and the bolt of the evening.
- Prayer is no mere exercise of words or of the ears; it is no mere repetition of empty formula.
- True prayer is not a prelude to inaction.
- Virtue lies in being absorbed in one's prayers in the presence of din and noise.
- Without prayer there is no inward melody.
- My greatest weapon is mute prayer.
- The meaning of prayer is that I want to evoke that divinity within me.
- Prayer has seen the saving of my life. Without it I should have been a lunatic long ago.
- Fasting and prayer are common injunctions in my religion.

- A personal selfish prayer is bad whether made before an image or an unseen God.
- Begin your day with prayer so that you may have a peaceful night free from dreams and nightmares.
- Empty prayer is like a 'sounding brass or a tinkling cymbal'.
- Buddhism is one long prayer.
- God answers prayer in His own way, not ours.

Preaching

- Preaching makes no appeal to me, and I get suspicious of missionaries who preach.
- I cannot say what to preach, but I can say that a life of service and uttermost simplicity is the best preaching.

Prison

- Our triumph consists in thousands being led to the prisons like lambs to the slaughter-house.
- By noiselessly going to prison, a civil resister ensures a calm atmosphere.

Progress

- In our progress towards the goal, we ever see more and more enchanting scenery.
- Friends were friends only when they helped one to progress in life.
- All education in a country has got to be demonstrably in promotion of the progress of the country in which it is given.

Prohibition

- I would rather have India without education, if that is the price to be paid for making it dry.
- A snake can only destroy the body, but the curse of drink corrupts the soul within.

Promise

If the promise inscribed in a promissory note is not honoured, the promissory note is worth nothing and fit only to be burnt to pieces and thrown away.

Propaganda

- Practice is the best speech and the best propaganda.
- No language can spread through mere propaganda.

Prophets

The prophets live and they die but their doctrines often fructify after centuries.

Public Opinion

- Performance of one's duty should be independent of public opinion.
- The only force at the disposal of democracy was that of the public opinion.

Punishment

- Punishment is God's who alone is the infallible Judge.
- No sin, no breach of Nature's law, goes unpunished.

Pure—Purity—Purification

- Pure motives can never justify impure or violent action.
- The purer I try to become, the nearer I feel to God.
- To a pure heart all hearts are pure.
- Waiting on God means increasing purity.
- Temple going is for the purification of the soul.
- God can never be realised by one who is not pure of heart.
- Every single act of one who would lead a life of purity should be in the nature of yagya.
- Tulsidas' Ramayana is a notable booth because it is informed with the spirit of purity, pity and piety.

- I should wish to die if a man who is impure should parade his purity in front of me.

Rama (Ramanama, Ram Raj)

- Ramanama is for the pure in heart and for those who want to attain purity and remain pure.
- Even Ramanama is by itself lifeless, but it has become a living symbol of the deity, because millions of people have consecrated it.

Reading

Reading comes before writing, and drawing before tracing the letters of the alphabet.

Realisation

- The freedom from all attachment is the realisation of God as truth.
- Divine knowledge is not borrowed from books. It has to be realised in oneself.

Reason

- In man, reason quickens and guides the feeling: in brute, the soul lies ever dormant.
- Faith is a kind of sixth sense which works in cases which are without the purview of reason.
- Faith becomes lame when it ventures into matters pertaining to reason.

Rebellion

Complete civil disobedience is a state of peaceful rebellion, a refusal to obey every single state-made law.

Reform (Reformer)

- A reformer's business is to make the impossible possible by giving an ocular demonstration of the possibility in

his own conduct.

• A reformer has to sail not with the current, often he has to go against it, even though it may cost him his life.

• You cannot achieve durable reform by becoming impatient.

Regularity

Unless the whole work is done with clockwork regularity, it is impossible to organise it in a thorough manner.

Religion

- Religion is one tree with many branches. As branches, you may say, religions are many, but as tree, religion is only one.
- Even as a tree has a single trunk, but many branches and leaves, there is one religion, but any number of faiths.
- Religions are different roads converging to the same point.
- God-given religion is beyond all speech.
- Religion should be dearer than life itself.
- Religion taught us to return good for evil.
- A religious act cannot be performed with aid of the bayonet or the bomb.
- Religion was entirely a personal matter. Each one could preach his creator as one liked.
- Religion is not like a house or a clock, which can be changed at will.
- All the great religions of the world inculcate the equality and brotherhood of mankind and the virtue of tolerance.
- Purest religion is highest expediency. Many things are lawful but they are not all expedient.
- No religion taught man to kill fellowman because he held different opinions or was of another religion.
- To befriend the one who regards himself as your enemy is the quintessence of religion.
- A man without a religion is like a ship without a rudder.

- Hypocrisy and distortion are passing currently under the name of religion.
- Where there is fear, there is no religion.
- I believe that religious education must be the sole concern of religious association.
- I desire no honour if I have to conceal my religious beliefs in order to have it.
- I have felt that the Gita teaches us that what cannot be followed out in day-to-day practice cannot be religion.
- It was through the Hindu religion that I learnt to respect Christianity and Islam.
- My religion is a matter solely between my maker and myself.
- My religion has no geographical limits.
- My religion is based on truth and non-violence. Truth is my God. Non-violence is the means of realising Him.
- My religion teaches me that a promise once made or a vow once taken for a worthy object may not be broken.
- My religion says that only he who is prepared to suffer can pray to God.
- My religion teaches me that whenever there is distress, which one cannot remove, one must fast and pray.
- My Hindu instinct tells me that all religions are more or less true.
- Fasting and prayer are common injunctions in my religion.
- Hinduism is not a codified religion.
- Hinduism is not an exclusive religion. There is room in it for the worship of all the prophets in the world.
- Hinduism with its message of ahimsa is to me the most glorious religion in the world.
- Dharma is one and one only, ahimsa means moksha, and moksha is the realisation of truth.
- Ahimsa is the height of Kshatriya dharma as it represents the climax of fearlessness.
- Belief in one God is the cornerstone of all religions.

- Truth is my religion and ahimsa is the only way of its realisation.
- "Do not worry in the least about yourself; leave all worry to God", this appears to be the commandment in all religions.
- No Indian who aspires to follow the way of true religion can afford to remain aloof from politics.
- Love is the basis of our friendship as it is of religion.
- Conversion without a clean heart is a denial of God and religion.
- The practice of truth and non-violence melted the religious differences, and we learnt to see beauty in each religion.

Renunciation

- Renunciation is everyone's prerogative.
- Renunciation means absence of hankering after fruit.
- The renunciation of the Gita is the acid test of faith.
- The secret of happy life lies in renunciation of life.
- Knowledge and devotion, to be true, have to stand the test of renunciation of the fruits of action.
- The sanyasa of the Gita will not tolerate complete cessation of activity.

Research

All research will be useless if it is not allied to internal research.

Resolution

More promises mean nothing, if there is not an unalterable resolution behind them.

Responsibility

Responsibility will mellow and sober the youth and prepare them for the burden they have to discharge.

Restraint

- Moral results can only be produced by moral restraints.
- Let India become alive by self-purification, that is, self-restraint and self-denial, and she will be a boon to herself and mankind.

Retaliation

Retaliation is a counter-poison; poison breeds more poison. The nectar of love alone can destroy the poison of hate.

Retirement

The old men should yield with grace what will be taken from them by force if they do not read the signs of the times.

Revolutionary

Impatience will blur the revolutionary's vision and lead him astray.

Rich

- Justice should become cheap and expeditious. Today it is the luxury of the rich and joy of the gambler.
- Let there be no distinction between rich and poor, high and low.
- I own no property and yet I feel that I am perhaps the richest man in the world.

Ridicule

Ridicule is like repression. Both give place to respect when they fail to produce the intended effect.

Right

- The true source of rights is duty.
- If we all discharge our duties, rights will not be far to seek.

- No people have risen who thought only of rights, only those did so who thought of duties.
- Out of the performance of duties flow rights, and those that knew and performed their duties came naturally by the rights.
- Passive resistance is a method of securing rights by personal suffering; it is the reverse of resistance by arms.
- Violence becomes imperative when an attempt is made to assert rights without any reference to duties.

Risk

If we want to overtake the storm, which is about to burst on us, we must take bolder risks and sail full steam ahead.

Rose

- The fragrance of religious and spiritual life is much finer and subtler than that of the rose.
- A rose does not need to preach. It simply spreads its fragrance. The fragrance is its own sermon.

Sacrifice

- A life of sacrifice is the pinnacle of art, and is full of true joy.
- God accepts the sacrifice of the pure in heart.
- Non-cooperation means nothing less than training in self-sacrifice.
- The Charkha is the symbol of sacrifice, and sacrifice is essential for the establishment of the image of the deity.
- Woman is the embodiment of sacrifice and suffering and her advent in public life should, therefore, result in purifying it, in restraining unbridled ambition and accumulation of property.
- Non-cooperation is a measure of discipline and sacrifice, and it demands respect for the opposite views.

Saint

- A saint who considers himself superior to a sinner forfeits his sainthood and becomes worse than the sinner, who unlike the proud saint knows not what he is doing.
- The temples are for the sinners, not for the saints.

Salt

- If salt loses its savour, wherewith can it be salted?
- There is no article like salt, outside water, by taxing which the state can reach the starving millions, the sick, the maimed and the utterly helpless.

Salvation

- Salvation is nothing more and nothing less than being well in every way.
- Moksha is a bodiless super physical state in which there is neither drinking nor eating and, therefore, neither the milking of buffalo nor the plucking even of a weed.

Sanitation

Corporate sanitation can only be ensured if there is a corporate conscience and a corporate insistence on cleanliness in public places.

Sanskrit

Every Hindu should have enough knowledge of Sanskrit to be able to express himself in that language.

Satan

- Satan's success is the greatest when he appears with the name of God on his lips.
- I am not likely to obtain the result flowing from the worship of God by laying myself prostrate before Satan.

- God rules even where Satan seems to hold sway, because the latter exists only on God's sufferance.

Satyagraha (Satyagrahi)

- Satyagraha is a process of educating public opinion, such that it covers all the elements of the society and in the end makes itself irresistible.
- Satyagraha is an attribute of the spirit within.
- Satyagraha has been designed as an effective substitute for violence.
- Satyagraha is itself an unmistakable mute prayer of organised soul.
- Satyagraha can rid society of all evils, political, economic and moral.
- Satyagraha and civil disobedience and fasts had nothing in common with the use of force, veiled or open.
- Satyagraha is a purely spiritual weapon.
- Satyagraha thrives on repression till at last the repressor is tired of it and the object of Satyagraha is gained.
- In Satyagraha, a courted imprisonment carries its own praise.
- Satyagraha does not depend on the outside help; it derives all its strength from within.
- In the dictionary of Satyagraha, there is no enemy.
- Since Satyagraha is a method of conversion and conviction, it seeks never to use the slightest coercion.
- It is claimed for Satyagraha that it is a complete substitute for violence or war.
- Satyagraha is a force that has come to stay. No force in the world can kill it.
- Satyagraha does not begin and end with civil disobedience.
- A clear victory of Satyagraha is impossible so long as there is ill-will.
- A Satyagrahi is sometimes bound to use language, which is capable of two meanings, provided both the meanings

are obvious and necessary and there is no intention to deceive anyone.

- A Satyagrahi has infinite patience, abundant faith in others and ample hope.
- A Satyagrahi has no other stay but God, and he who has any other stay or depends on any other help cannot offer Satyagraha.
- A Satyagrahi has always his minimum and it is the minimum that is wanted in connection with this struggle.
- The Satyagrahi should not have any hatred in his heart against the opponent.
- A Satyagrahi is dead to his body even before the enemy attempts to kill him.
- To die without killing is the badge of a Satyagrahi.
- A Satyagrahi lays down his life, but never gives up that is the meaning of the 'do or die' slogan.

Schools

All our national schools ought to be converted into factories of our national ammunition, namely, constructive work.

Science

- Science to be science must afford the fullest scope for satisfying the hunger of body, mind and soul.
- To state the limitation of science is not to belittle it.
- Scientific knowledge requires constant probing into the why and wherefore of every little process that you perform.
- Ahimsa is a science. The word 'failure' has no place in the vocabulary of science.

Scriptures

- A prayerful study and experience are essential for a correct interpretation of the scriptures.
- A man, who would interpret the scriptures, must have the spiritual discipline.
- Every true scripture only gains by criticism.

Self

Searching of self ennobles, searching of others debases.

Self-confidence

The history of the world is full of instances of men who rose to leadership by sheer force of self-confidence, bravery and tenacity.

Self-control

A votary of ahimsa must cultivate a habit of unremitting toil, sleepless vigilance and ceaseless self-control.

Self-defence

- The strength to kill is not essential for self-defence, one ought to have the strength to die.
- Self-defence is the only honourable course where there is unreadiness for self-immolation.

Self-immolation

Not even self-immolation can be allowed to support a bad or an immoral cause.

Selflessness

Selflessness may be the present form of selfishness.

Self-pity

Self-pity comes when you do a thing for which you expect recognition from others.

Self-realisation

- Life is an aspiration. Its mission is to strive after perfection which is self-realisation.
- There is no other way of self-realisation except the way of complete self-abandonment.

Self-respect

- Man does not live by bread alone. Many prefer self-respect to food.
- Self-respect and honour cannot be protected by others. They are for each individual himself or herself to guard.

Self-restraint

Self-restraint is the very keystone of the ethics of vow-taking.

Self-sacrifice

Self-sacrifice of one innocent man is a million times more potent than the sacrifice of a million men who die in the act of killing others.

Service

- Service is not possible unless it is rooted in love or ahimsa.
- The platform of services is as big as the world. It is never overcrowded.
- My creed is service of God and, therefore, of humanity.
- Human body is meant solely for service, never for indulgence.
- Charkha is an instrument of service.
- Man becomes not the lord and master of all creation, but he is its servant.
- This belief in the necessity of English training has enslaved us. It has unfitted us for true national service.
- Man's triumph will consist in substituting the struggle for existence by the struggle for mental service.

Silence

- Silence is a great help to a seeker after truth like me.
- Experience has taught me that silence is part of the spiritual discipline of a votary of truth.
- Modern civilisation has taught us to convert night into

day and golden silence into brazen din and noise.

Simplicity

Simplicity is the essence of universality.

Slave (Slavery)

To end slavery, you must overcome the mental and physical inertia of the masses and quicken their intelligence and creative faculty.

Teacher

- What does Jesus mean to me? To me, He was one of the greatest teachers humanity has ever had.
- No teacher can be held responsible for a caricature of his teachings.

Temples

- I know of no religion or sect that has done or is doing without its house of God, variously described as a temple, a mosque, a church or a synagogue.
- I hold it a blasphemy to say that the creator resides in a temple from which a particular class of His devotees sharing the faith in it is excluded.
- It is necessary first to purify the drunken and dissolute worshippers in charge of some of these temples.
- The temples were like spiritual hospitals, and the sinful, which were spiritually diseased, had the first right to be ministered unto by them.
- Temples are meant for sinners where they can wash away their sins.

Terrorism

Terrorism and deception are weapons not of the strong but of the weak.

Thoughts

- Deeds are indifferent caricatures of our thoughts.
- Thought is never complete unless it finds expression in action and action limits your thought.

Time

- Time is always on the side of those who will wait upon it.
- Truth alone will endure, all the rest will be swept away before the tide of time.

Tolerance

- Tolerance gives us spiritual insight, which is as far from fanaticism as the North Pole is from the south.
- Tolerance obviously does not disturb the distinction between right and wrong, or good and evil.
- The first step in non-violence is that we cultivate in our daily life, as between ourselves, truthfulness humility, tolerance and loving kindness.

Tools

It is a bad carpenter who quarrels with his tools. It is a bad general who blames his men for faulty workmanship.

Trust

- Trustworthy action will dispel all mistrust or distrust as the sun dispels the morning mist.
- Trusting one another, however, can never mean trusting with the lip and mistrusting in the heart.

Truth

- Truth is what the voice within tells you.
- Truth is the right designation of God.
- Truth and ahimsa will never be destroyed.
- Truth is like a vast tree which yields more and more fruit

the more you nurture it.

- The quest of truth involves tapasya (self-suffering) sometimes even unto death.
- Though God may be Love, God is Truth above all.
- God alone is truth and everything else is transitory and illusory.

- God of truth and justice can never create distinctions of high and low among his own children.
- If you would swim on the bosom of the ocean of truth, you must reduce yourself to a zero.
- Nobody in this world possesses absolute truth.
- Search for truth is search for God. Truth is God. God is because truth is.
- A man with a grain of faith in God never loses hope, because he ever believes in the ultimate triumph of truth.
- We do not enter the kingdom of liberty with mere lip-homage to truth and non-violence.
- I know no diplomacy save that of truth.
- I acknowledge not other God but the one God of truth and righteousness.
- My experience teaches me that truth can never be propagated by doing violence.
- My religion is based on truth and non-violence. Truth is God. Non-violence is the means of realising Him.
- Let hundreds like me perish, but let the truth triumph.
- Our life is a long quest after truth, and the soul requires restfulness to attain its full height.
- Buddha renounced all worldly happiness because he wanted to share with the whole world his happiness, which was to be had by men who sacrificed and suffered in the search for truth.
- Ahimsa and Truth are so intertwined that it is practically impossible to disentangle and separate them.

Understanding

- Reason has to be strengthened by suffering and suffering

opens the eyes of undertaking.

- Three-fourths of the miseries and understandings in the world will disappear, if we step into the shoes of our adversaries and understand their standpoint.

Unity

- Unity among the different races and the different communities belonging to different religions of India is indispensable to the birth of national life.
- My motto is: 'unite now today if you can, fight if you must, but in every case avoid British intervention'.

University

- The aim of university education should be to turn out true servants of the people, who would live and die for the country's freedom.
- A university never needs a pile of majestic buildings and treasures of gold and silver. What it does need most of all is the intelligent backing of public opinion.

Untouchability

- Untouchability is a hydra-headed monster.
- Untouchability is a terrible reality.
- The removal of untouchability is one of the highest expressions of ahimsa.
- God never made man that he may consider another man as an untouchable.
- If untouchability lives, humanity must die.
- My fight against untouchability is a fight against the impure in humanity.
- We shall dig our own grave if we do not purge ourselves of this curse of untouchability.
- Hinduism dies if untouchability lives, and untouchability has to die if Hinduism is to live.
- It is a crime and a sin to regard a person as untouchable

because he is born in a particular community.

- To say that a single human being, because of his birth, becomes an untouchable, unapproachable or invisible, is to deny God.
- No stone shall be left unturned to bring home to the family members that untouchability is a sin and a blot on Hinduism.
- The purification required is not of untouchables but of the so-called superior castes.

Untruth

- Truth and untruth often co-exist; good and evil are often found together.
- The error does not become truth by reason of multiplied propagation, nor does truth become error because nobody sees it.
- A man of God never strives after untruth and, therefore, he can never lose hope.

Utility

The amount of public support that an institution can command affords a true measure of its utility.

Vedas

The Vedas are as indefinable as God and Hinduism.

Vegetarianism

The correct way for the people to spread vegetarianism is to reason out its bounties, which should be exhibited in their lives.

Victory

The greater our innocence, the greater our strength and the swifter is our victory.

Villages

- Healthy and nourishing food was the only alpha and omega of rural economy.
- If we want to impart education best suited to the needs of the villagers, we should take the vidyapith to the villages.
- Real India lives in villages.

Violence (Himsa)

- I hold that the world is sick of armed rebellions.
- It is my firm conviction that nothing enduring is built on violence.
- My dictionary has no such expression as a violent fight.
- Between violence and cowardly fight, I can only prefer violence to cowardice.
- I cannot teach you violence, as I do not myself believe in it. I can only teach you not to bow your heads before any one even at the cost of your life.
- My experience teaches me that truth can never be propagated by doing violence.
- I do not regard killing or assassination or terrorism as good in any circumstance whatsoever.
- Violence becomes imperative when an attempt is made to assert rights without any reference to duties.
- What is gained by violence must be lost before superior violence.
- If there is violence, it will certainly be crushed because violence can only end in a disgraceful soul.
- A successful bloody revolution can only mean further misery for the masses.
- Where there is only a choice between cowardice and violence, I would advise violence.
- India's freedom will not be won by violence only but by the purest suffering without retaliation.
- The man who uses coercion is guilty of deliberate violence. Coercion is inhuman.
- Non-violence is an unchangeable creed. It has to be

pursued even in the face of violence raging around you.

- When the panchayat raj is established, public opinion will do what violence can never do.
- When there is no desire for fruit, there is also no temptation for untruth or himsa.

Virtue

Non-violence is not merely a personal virtue. It is also a social virtue to be cultivated like the other virtues.

Vow

- A vow imparts stability, ballast and firmness to one's character.
- It goes without saying that moderation and sobriety are of the very essence of vow-taking.

War

- War knows no law except that of might.
- History is a record of perpetual wars, but we are trying to make new history.
- Non-violence requires more than the courage of the soldier of war.
- A warrior lives on his wars, whether offensive or defensive. He suffers a collapse if he finds that his warring capacity is unwanted.

Waste

You may not waste a grain of rice or a scrap of paper, and similarly a minute of your time. It is not ours. It belongs to the nation and we are trustees for the use of it.

Wealth

A man's true wealth hereafter is the good he has done to his fellowmen.

Widow (Widowhood)

- To coerce widowhood upon little girls is a brutal crime for which we Hindus are daily paying dearly.
- Every widow I have met has recognised in the wheel a dear forgotten friend.
- Khaddar brings a ray of hope to the widow's broken-up home.

Woman

- Woman is the incarnation of ahimsa. Ahimsa means infinite love, which again means infinite capacity for suffering.
- Woman is, by habit or nature, queen of the household. She is not designed to organise on a large scale.
- Women are special custodians of all that is pure and religious in life.
- A fearless woman who knows that her purity is her best shield can never be dishonoured.
- There is no occasion for women to consider them subordinate or inferior to men.
- Woman is the companion of man, gifted with equal mental capacities.
- Languages proclaim that woman is half of man, and by parity of reasoning, man is half of woman.

Work

- Joint work is impossibility where the workers distrust one another.
- Lack of finances never represented a real difficulty to a sincere worker. Finances follow; they dog your foot-steps if you represent a real cause.
- The whole world is like the human body with its various members. Pain in one organ is felt in the whole body.
- The greatest menace to the world today is the growing, exploiting irresponsible imperialism.
- An India awakened and free has a message of peace and

goodwill to a groaning world.

- Love is the subtlest force in the world.
- The world is changing every moment and is, therefore, unreal. It has non-permanent existence.
- The world can't be successfully fooled for all time.
- It is indeed a million times better to appear untrue before the world than to be untrue to ourselves.

Worship

- Some form of common worship and a common place of worship appear to be a human necessity.
- God is omnipresent; even a pebble in River Narmada can represent Him and serve as an object of worship.

Yagya

- Yagya is not yagya if one feels it to be burdensome or annoying.
- Yagya is duty to be performed or service to be rendered, all twenty-four hours of the day.

□

References

Books

1. Complete Works of Gandhi
2. ind Swaraj by M.K. Gandhi
3. The Story of My Experiments with Truths by M.K. Gandhi
4. The Teaching of the Gita by M.K. Gandhi

Websites

1. brainyquote.com
2. famousquotes.com
3. freeindia.org
4. gandhi-manibhavan.org
5. gandhiserve.org
6. mahatma.com
7. mahatmagandhi.org
8. mkgandhi-sarvodaya.org
9. mkgandhi.org
10. poetseers.org
11. quotationpage.com
12. wikipedia.org
13. wikiquote.org
14. worldofquotes.com

□□□